LOVE HAS WINGS
INTO THE UNKNOWN

LOVE HAS WINGS INTO THE UNKNOWN

MAMATA DEY

PARTRIDGE

A Penguin Random House Company

To order additional copies of this book, contact
Partridge India
000 800 10062 62
orders.india@partridgepublishing.com

www.partridgepublishing.com/india

To my husband

INTRODUCTION

Ravi and Sheela are childhood friends and live in a small town of Odisha and when they enter into their teens, they realize they are in love with each other. When Ravi reaches the age of fifteen, he loses his parents in an accident by a strange quirk of misfortune. His uncle comes and takes him back to his native place which is Kerala. Overcome by the greed of property, Ravi's uncle stops his education and sends him to the Arab countries to work as a labourer, while his sister, who is older to him is forcibly married off to an elderly person. Thus Ravi is separatd from Sheela. In the meantime, Sheela's parents get her married to a low-paid, plump Govt. employee and Ravi is married to an MLA's (politician) daughter. Twenty years pass away. The story begins with Sheela visiting a fair which is annually held in the town where her father used to stay during her childhood. She spots Ravi in the fair, recognizes him and rushes forward to meet him, but is unable to contact him there. But somehow, she comes to know that he is working in a particular bank in Mumbai and she writes to him with his half-address on the envelope. Fortunately, the letter reaches Ravi's hands and their old flame of love is revived. Thus begins an extra-marital affair between them, unknown to their respective spouses. They secretly meet in parks and beaches and consummate their love in hotel rooms.

After some days of this secret enjoyment of their love, Sheela's mother-in-law has to undergo a major operation. Circumsatnces compel the lovers to be together in a hotel room while the operation is going on in the nursing home, and they unknowingly and unwillingly become witnesses in a rape case which has happened in the adjacent room to their room in the hotel. In the courtroom, they speak the truth and based on their witness, the supposed-to-be rapist is acquitted of the charge; but fortunately or unfortunately, the lovers become victims of the prosecutors who try to kill them. **In a bid to escape, they land high up in the Himalayas, in a strange world ruled and lorded by a Godman. They become his disciples and in the clean, pure and fresh air and ambience, they fully enjoy the blissful feeling of love and togetherness for two years when all of a sudden, the Godman's beautiful daughter comes from a foreign land, falls in love with Ravi(alias Anand) and wishes to marry him. But Ravi rejects her proposal and rushes back to his dearest Sheela(alias Anandi). Ultimately, Ravi and Sheela die happily in each others' arms, after being shot at by the Godman who is forced to do so due to love for his daughter.**

1

Ravi was working on his computer that rainy afternoon at half-past three when the peon brought in some letters. He glanced at them and thought there would be some important information regarding his project. As he threw them one by one on the table, one particular envelope caught his attention. He could sense a far-off familiarity in the hand which had written his half-address on it. The envelope seemed heavy. Anyway, he didn't have the time to flip open the envelope and read on; he thought he would read it during lunch-break. But as he clicked the mouse, his eyeballs wavered from the computer screen to the envelope on the table. Somehow he could not concentrate. Something in him urged him to read the letter he tore it open.

"My dearest, dearest darling.!" He was flabbergasted. Who could it be! Certainly not his wife! A tinge of excitement surged through his entire body. Hopes of an extra-marital affair interested him. He read on. "A bomb has been dropped on you." Strange, thought Ravi. Darling, and then bomb! "Its not a terrorist bomb which will destroy you. It's a beloved's bomb which will give you a new life, a fresh life, a vibrant and wouderful life. Like a phoenix, you'll rise up from a dull, drab and ashy-grey world to a new, rosy, bright, love-lustre world. My love, please don't be bored; hold on your interest for a little longer. I'm coming to the point just now.".

Ravi paused. Yes, he just remembeed. It was Sheela's. Somewhere, in the innermost recesses of his mind, memories of her lurked now and then. But he had deliberately quelled them, knowing well enough that indulging in such thoughts would only be a fruitless pleasure. He read on: "The fact is that just a month ago, I caught a glimpse of you in that fair which is annually held in that cute little town called Chandnagar, near Bhubaneswar. O, what a quaint little town it was then, where we spent most of our childhood, roaming about in its busy, crowded and congested lanes and bylanes, sucking chocolates and licking icecreams. It was wonderful, wasn't it, my dear. Then love was there, everywhere, in our hearts and in the air, here and there and everywhere, in our homes and and in the fair. O yes, coming to the fair, the place was so crowded and there was so much noise that you didn't hear me calling you from just a few feet away. Desperately, I tried to reach you, butyou were just a mirage in the sea of human beings. Each time I saw you from afar, I rushed to reach you even while jostling amongst the crowd, and the moment I thought I had reached you, you just vanished into thin air. At a particular moment, I thought I had got you, but just then, my little son pulled me away, "Mama, mama, I want that toy car, please", and I was distracted. And then you got lost amidst the crowd. I returned home and wept bitterly that night. Why is it that fate always snatches you away from me? That's what I thought and felt sad about. But then, I did not want to be defeated this time. The following day, I set about searching for you or your address. In that small town, I remembered that an aunt of yours lived in Gehna Bazaar, and I scooted to her house. She didn't know that you had come to Chandnagar and she said that probably I had mistaken someone else for you. I inwardly laughed at her folly! How could she know that your face was imprinted in my heart and soul and eyes too and I could never make a mistake where you were concerned. Anyway, she didn't know your residential address; but she informed me that you were working in a particular branch of Canara Bank in Mumbai, and that's how this letter has reached you. Well, I don't know whether you still love me or not; but one thing is certain, I love you and will keep on loving you throughout my life. If not lovers since both of us are married, at least we can be friends. Anyway, I would love to meet you, talk to you, and revive the good old days of yesteryears. If you feel the same about me, kindly ring me up at this number—23489672, preceeding it with Kolkata code, between 12 noon and 3p.m I live at Kolkata with my husband and son.

> With lots and lots of love,
> Up hill and down dale,
> Yours, Sheela."

Wow! Great! My lovely Sheela. Thursting his head backwards and looking up at the ceiling, he went back in time. Yes, he remembered her sweetness, her innocence and warmth as a teenager, and felt suffused with a peculiar glow within his whole body. Love and romance, which had sedimented to the bottom of his mind, resurfaced again and he felt young and vibrant. He looked at his watch. It was already nearing 4 p.m. Then he glanced at the letter. She had written between 12 noon and 3 p. m. It would be wise to wait till the next day to make a call.

2

That night Ravi could not sleep well. Images of his childhood and teenage years flashed into his mind now and then, and he remembered how loving and affectionate Sheela and her parents were. He and his parents had come into their neighbourhood as tenants, when he was only three years old, and his father, being a central govt railway employee had been transferred to that town. Sheela's parents had rushed forward to help them in every possible way and make them feel at home in that new and strange place. Thus the foundation of a strong and abiding friendship between the two families had been laid. At that time, Sheela was only two years old and like her parents, she had taken to their family immediately, and very often toddled to their house in order to play with Ravi. Since then, they became inseparable companions and when the time came for Ravi to take admission in a good English medium school, Sheela also went with him and took admission in the same class, though she was a year younger. Thus, Sheela became his classmate too, and as Ravi put back the clock, he recollected with fond memories how wonderful and joyous those days were.

A groan and a loud snore from his wife brought him back to the present. Well, Sheela too must have missed him all these years and pined for him, or else why would she write this letter.? Now and then, when thoughts of Sheela had invaded his mind, he had thwarted it away thinking she must have forgotten about him. But no! He felt glad that memories of him were still alive and fresh in her mind and now, all of a sudden, in his thirty-fifth year, the prospect of love opened up green avenues of joy in his mind, and his heart vibrated to a whole new world of colour and romance. He realised with vibrancy that love had been rekindled in him and he became madly anxious to talk with Sheela and meet her.

He would definitely ring her up after 12 noon, and the next day, while in his office, it seemed to him twelve o'clock would never come. At last, it did come and his cell on the table looked up at him tantalizingly as if daring him to pick it up and make a call. He grabbed it and looking at the envelope in front, he clicked the numbers. But alas, to no avail.! Damn it, the battery's electric charge had run out. O, what to do!. Quickly, he rushed to the landline, but the phone was out of order. O no! Why is it that the things we want the most never come to us easily; he felt infuriated. But he was not to be outdone. The peon was coming that way. "Raju, give me your cell please, just for a minute."

"O Sir, please forgive me. I feel ashamed that I can't help you because there's very little balance left. Only Rs. 3/-."

"Never mind! I'll give you Rs 50/- for recharging. Just give me now. Rs3/- will suffice." Ravi desperately wanted to ring up. He clicked the numbers.

"Hello!" a gruff, rude, male voice greeted him.

Ravi remained silent for a moment. He was sure he had clicked the right numbers. Then why hadn't Sheela picked up the phone? It was already half-past twelve in the afternoon. Probably it was her husband.

"Hello! Who is it?" the same voice again.

Ravi wanted to say "Is this Mrs. Sheela Bannerjee's house?" but he withheld himself. It would give rise to unnecessary suspicion. On the spur of the moment, he invented an unnecessary question. He asked "Is this the LIC office?"

"No". The voice blared loudly at the other end. "Wrong number. And a piece of advice for you, mister. Don't click up wrong nos. again." And the person banged the receiver on the phone.

How could Sheela be so idiotic? Ravi thought. Writing to him she'd be there at home between 12 noon-3p.m and not being there. But how was Ravi to know that by chance that day, her husband had returned from office exactly at 12.05 p.m. because he had forgotten some important file; and by some quirk of misfortune, he had received Ravi's call. After that, Mr Bannerjee had a sumptuous lunch cooked by Sheela and fell into a siesta. Ravi rang up again at half-past two in the afternoon. He felt sure Sheela would pick up the phone this time. The ringing woke up Mr. Bannerjee's siesta and he looked at his watch. "O my God, it's already nearing three o'clock. I have to hurry." Then he picked up the receiver. "Hello!" Ravi's voice paused anxiously. "Oh! It's you again. That LIC man! I told you this is not the LIC office. And who the hell are you to disturb a peaceful man like me. Henceforth, stop this nonsense!" And Mr. Bannerjee banged the receiver again.

Ravi couldn't make head or tail of this whole episode. So many questions troubled him. Had Sheela given him a wrong number? Why would she give him a wrong number? Was she playing a joke on him? No, no, Sheela wasn't like that. She was so earnest about everything. Was that man who received her phone her husband.? If so, Sheela must be leading a miserable life. However, he would ring up the next day. The following day, it was a Wednesday; just when he was about to click the numbers after getting some respite from the bank's customers at half-past twelve, The GM called for him. There was an important meeting and Ravi remained tied to his chair till 4p.m. He dare not ring up at any other time other than what was mentioned by Sheela in her letter, lest the air of suspicion would blow and his hopes of love and romance would be nipped in the bud instead of blossoming and flowering

On the other side, Sheela anxiously waited for his call from the tenth day onwards after she had sent her letter. But when no calls came from Ravi, she felt sure that the letter hadn't reached him at all. So on Thursday, confident that she would miss no call from Ravi, at one o'clock in the afternoon, she went to buy some vegetables when she saw that there was none at home for the night meal. Just then, Ravi found a little respite from his laborious work, and checking the time on his watch which read 1.05p.m, he clicked on the numbers on his cell. The land phone rang and rang and there was no answer. Sheela returned at half-past one from the market and sat down exhausted and very dissappointed too. What if Ravi had received the letter, but no longer loved her and therefore did not call her on the phone? She decided she would write to him again. On Friday, it rained very heavily and a mini-cyclone rocked the whole city of Mumbai. The telephone network had collapsed. Ravi cursed his luck. The next day at one o'clock, Ravi decided he would make a last attempt. The day being Saturday, a half-day, Sheela's husband had picked up his son from school at 12 noon and had brought him home. He was taking his lunch when the phone rang. "Hello!" Ravi said over enthusiastically, hoping and praying that Sheela would pick up the phone.

"O, it's you again, the LIC man." Sheela's husband growled." How dare you disturb me like this." Ravi was at his wits'end. He did not know what to say. However, very level-headedly, he said "Sir, forgive me, I'm an LIC agent and I want to make a policy of yours.

"But how did you know me?"

"I had visited your office once and they told me you had no LIC policy. Sir, please help me by making a small policy."

"Help you, my foot! On the one hand you disturb me at every odd hour; on the other hand, I don't have enough money for savings, what with my wife and son to look after, and my sisters and mother in the village dependant on me. I certainly won't make any policy. And mind you, never disturb me again. If you do, I'll go the the BSnl office and find out your number and sue you for making unnecessary phone calls." Sheela's husband threatened and put down the receiver.

Ravi felt miserable—he couldn't contact Sheela. He was wary of ringing up to her again lest her husband or whoever he was really filed up a legal case against him. And he did not want to enter into hassles where Sheela was concerned. However, he still hoped to meet her someday in the near future, for already Sheela had started the process of finding about his whereabouts after so many years. And he was sure she wouldn't give up so easily.

Meanwhile, Sheela's heart sank within herself more and more when she waited anxiously for Ravi's call, and no call came. Hers was a loveless life ever since Ravi had gone away from her teen years, for her parents though full of love and affection for her, were too busy bringing her up through her teenage and ladyhood and never cared to understand her feelings so well as Ravi did ;and marriage to an unfeeling log had worsened her woes. She had hoped that letter would be the key to some sort of relief from her lacklustre life; and then she thought with dismay that the letter probably hadn't reached Ravi at all. Or did Ravi receive it and was indifferent about it? Or had he forgotten about her or wanted to forget about her? Well, she would express her feelings this time; her love for him, her pain and suffering, the myriad experiences life had taught her and remind him of all their past days. Perhaps he would relent on knowing her heart and mind and make a call. She decided to write to him again praying fervently to God that the letter would reach him.

Dearest Ravi,

When I think of you, my heart beats with joy. I don't know or care to know whether you love me or not, but I feel great pleasure in just loving

15

you, or dreaming of you or imagining you. You are in my heart forever. At times, when I see the happiness of others, I feel pangs of jealousy stabbing at my heart, but soon I try to get over the feeling by trying to avoid thoughts about it. Why should I feel pained unnecessarily? For haven't you advised all along when we were teenagers that whenever I look up to see how many people are better off than us, I should also look down to see how many people are worse off. And that I should thank God and be happy with whatever he has given me; for everything is temporary, whether joy or sorrow and everything shall pass away. My dear, putting the clock back, I realise how mature and level-headed you were even at that young age. I sometimes think—is human life really worth worrying about? Just a bubble, so insignificant, mere breath, only air! A moment passes away and this life of ours becomes shorter. So why not enjoy that moment? And now I want to enjoy every moment, imagining you, thinking of you, and if possible, be near you. You remember, the time when we were kids. How we used to play together in the long, lazy, wintry afternoon sun along with other children of the neighborhood, and we would continue to play long after the evening shadows had lengthened and the sun would set. And then we would go home and be mildly rebuked by our parents as to why we hadn't sat down to study. And then, long after the sun would set, and the evening lamps be lit and the prayers would be recited, we would sit down with our books. I was always a very good student and I had to help with your homework. How much I loved to boss over you and when you couldn't do the sums, you used to sulk. But then, when we were together, love was there, everywhere, in my heart and in the air, everywhere, everywhere and these bossing and sulking just vanished away with the wind. Many things dear, I haven't told anyone, but I'm baring out my soul to you; Maybe you'll feel bored, but I have the right to bore you, havn't I, my dear? Many times I used to dream that I would be with you forever, but when it didn't happen, I felt a void within me, a despair, a hopelessness which became unbearable at times. And therefore I'm scared of dreaming, of hoping. You remember those times darling, when we had just entered into our teens, we used to sit upstairs throughout the long lazy afternoons, where the carpenter would be sawing his wood, humming a tune to himself. Then, we used to sing Hindi film songs at the top of our voice to drown the sawing sound and in our hearts of heart, we dreamt that we would always sing and sail along the river of life together. But it didn't happen. My dream was dashed to the ground. And again, when you were gone, I thought I would study hard, take competetive exams, and either get into a bank or a govt. job, or even a lecturership, so that I would be independent enough financially to search for you, find you and marry you, but that was not to be. For some years, I worked very hard, burning the midnight oil, taking exam after exam, praying all the while "O God, let me get through this time, at least", but that never happened. If I qualified in the written, I was rejected in the viva voce. With what hopes I faced the interview, but it always ended in dissappointment. When I saw my batchmates and friends, who were never so good as me in studies either in school or college, getting into lucrative and prestigous jobs like O.A.S, and probationary officers, the sword of envy stabbed at my heart and I could feel pain coursing through my veins. It was terrible, seeing others so well off in life, and me wallowing in misery. At such times, how I wished you were near me, for I was sure you would pull me out of this depression. And then my parents decided to get me married to this not-so-young man. I dreamt of love and romance, of a beautiful world with a loving husband but those dreams never turned into a reality. My mother-in-law ill-treated me for bringing in very little dowry. My husband was a typical mama's boy and never tried to understand me or support me. He seemed to derive a sadistic pleasure in belittling me in their opinion. For two years I couldn't produce a child. I felt they cursed me for being a barren wasteland, infertile, bereft of the seed and shower of love and affection. How would they know that I hardly had sex with my husband. And then, after two years and two months, in a fit of passion, my son was conceived in the fourth sexual act with my husband. And then, almost after three years of marriage, my son was born—what a bundle of joy! Life for me has changed since then. It's a tremendous pleasure mingled with great joy bringing him up and spending time with him—my dear dear son. And now when I find you, my happiness will be complete. But dear, I had dreamt of so many beautiful things, but none of those dreams came true. I'm afraid to dream any longer; in fact, I've forgotten to dream for its painful to tolerate the shattering of dreams. I've learnt to accept things as they are. If this letter finds and you still don't respond, at least I'll have the pleasure of knowing that I have bared my heart and soul to you. But, my dear, if you thinking of calling, ring me up between 12 noon and 3 p.m. any day of the week, excepting Saturday and Sunday at the same number which I given you in the previous letter

With lots and lots of love,
Yours forever,
Sheela.

3

The letter reached the bank in which Ravi worked. after ten days. The letter looked soiled, but a surge of joy swept up in him as he recognised Sheela's handwriting. He could know that the letter had touched and travelled through several branches of the bank before it had reached him. Anxiety had caused him sleepless nights these few days because he could not discover any road by means of which he could contact Sheela. The previous letter had ignited love in him. He wanted the flames to keep on burning and never to be put out. He snatched it from the peon's hand and quickly tore and read it. He felt absolutely delighted as though he was swimming in an ocean of joy. He looked at his watch. It was only half-past twelve. He recollected the phone no and clicked it on his cell praying fervently that Sheela would receive it and no one else and his prayers were answered.

Luckily, that day, Sheela was frying potato chips in the kitchen when the telephone rang. Somehow, she instinctively knew it was Ravi's. She picked up the receiver with trepidation and helloed nervously.

"Sheela, my dear," Ravi cried out excitedly. "how wondeful! We are together again after so many years. How much have I missed you all these years, my darling." Sheela could sense a tinge of pain in his overjoyous voice, even as tears of happiness coursed down her cheeks.

"Ravi!" Her voice was feeble and choked with emotion. "Thank God, the letter reached you. I was all the while praying that it would, for I feared that it woukd get missed." And then her voice strengthened and became louder. "O Ravi, I'm so glad that I've got you again. You were in my heart and mind all these days." And she wept a bit. Ravi could sense it.

"Sheela, what's this! Why are you crying? You know I never liked to see you in tears."

"O Ravi, these are only tears of happiness." Sheela tried to sound as cheerful as possible. "You know my joy is unbounded." She wiped off her tears with the ends of her sari. "Anyway, where are you? In your office?"

"Yes, and I've lots of pending work too. Nevertheless, I feel very relaxed today. It seems that a great load has been lifted out of my mind. I don't know why, but I feel very light-hearted today. Perhaps at the prospect of seeing you soon. A fortnight ago, for three days almost, I kept ringing you up several times, and I think the person who received it is your husband. Gosh! What a devil of a man really.! I'm sure you won't mind my telling this. And what a banging he gave me, man! I daren't ring you after that lest I may lose you once again. On receiving your second letter, I picked up the courage. I do so love your letters, dear. Anyway, please tell me when I can meet you. Make it as quickly as possible."

"But Ravi, when you came to Chandnagar last month, didn't old memories resurface in your mind? You could have at least enquired about me or my parents."

"Sheela, my dear, I had only gone for one day on a bank inspection My flight was on the same day at 9 p.m. After the inspection, the branch manager took me to the fair, not only to please me, but also to pass my time. Be assured that whether I'm in your hometown or anywhere else in the world, you are in my subconscious always. And I want to meet you as quickly as possible."

"Why don't you come down to Kolkata?"

"Right, good idea! Sometimes, I go there on some bank work, or to attend some meetings. By the way, I'm supposed to go there sometime during the next week. Tomorrow, exactly at this time, I'll ring you up to let you know where and when we can meet."

"Wonderful! I'm dying to meet you, Ravi. I'll be waiting for your call tomorrow. Just now, I suppose you have a lot of work, and I don't want to disturb you further. Should we end our talk here? My potato fry is getting burnt."

"Wow, what an anti-climax! Just like you, Sheela. Just when we are about to reach the peak of excitement, you fall down to dull boredom. Well, well, you haven't changed ; still very practical. Okay, as you say, my love." And Ravi switched off his cell-phone.

The next day was Friday. Ravi rang up from his cabin hoping that Sheela would receive it and no one else. Sheela once again helloed sweetly from the other end. "Sheela, I can't chat with you much today because there are plenty of customers here demanding my time and attention. But I'm seeing you on Monday sure, i.e. three days from now. I'll be waiting for you at the Howrah station, right outside the platform."

"But Ravi, the station is too far from our house. I think somewhere nearer will be convenient."

"Then quickly think of an appropriate venue."

"I can't. I leave it to you, Ravi."\

"Right! Then come somewhere near the Grand Hotel. I'm sure you can spot me near some shop or under a tree. Won't you recognize me, my dear? You see, a long twenty years have passed away and we haven't seen each other. Isn't it exciting, meeting after so many years! I hope you recognize me"

"Really Ravi, I think you can sometimes go to extremities in your joking. As if I can't recognise you! I think it's you who will not recognize me."

"Sheela, that's impossible! I can even sense your heartbeat, you're so close to me, my dear. Well, leaving aside these, let's come to the point. I'll be there exactly at half-past one. Meet me between 1.30 and 2 o'clock in the afternoon. Shall I ring you up tomorrow just to be further sure?"

"No, no! Tomorrow being Saturday, my husband maybe at home in the afternoon. Rest assured, I'll definitely meet you at the appointed place and time on Monday. Next, when we meet."

"Wow, Sheela! You sound so official and down-to-earth. But I'm sure, at heart you are still the same lady whom I love. Well, more when we meet on Monday. Till then, bye bye!" He switched off and Sheela put down the receiver with an ache in her heart. How much she loved and enjoyed talking with him, and now he had stopped. Her soul contracted. But then, she would meet him soon. There was a void, an emptiness in her mind and heart with which she had been living, and she now felt as though that void was beginning to fill up.

4

On Monday, Sheela was just in the seventh heaven of delight at the prospect of meeting Ravi after a gap of so many years. She felt very excited, though jittery of course, but she dare not show it on her face. She tried hard to concentrate on her usual household chores, and took extra care that her husband should not be displeased with her wifely duties, but at times her absent-minded expression gave way. "What's wrong with you, Sheela. You seem distracted these days!" Her husband remarked. "its nothing!" Sheela blushed and ran inside the kitchen pretending that the curry was getting overcooked. Not in his wildest imagination did her husband ever think that Sheela was going to meet her long-lost lover. How could he know that Sheela yearned to be loved and not just treated as an object.? He was a man devoid of passion and feeling, a male chauvinist who thought that a woman's salvation lay only in looking after the well-being of her husband or her brother or her son. But Sheela longed to feel wanted, to be caressed and kissed; and her twelve-year old marriage was completely shorn of love, in which she had been just a repressed, suppressed and oppressed wife. She was sure Ravi would replenish all that she had lost by marriage.

Came the D-time when she would meet Ravi! After her husband had gone to the office at 10.30 a. m., she tidied up the kitchen and had a refreshing bath with soap and warm water lest her body smelt of spices. She had also shampooed her hair and after running it through a drier, she sprayed on herself a sweet-smelling deo. She dressed up, draping on herself a lovely sari with a matching blouse. Then she glanced at the mirror and thought "do I really look beautiful?" The reflection answered back that she was indeed lovely. A bob of shiny, glossy black hair framed her fair and oval face and fell to her shoulders, while her model-like figure was draped in an emerald-green sari with white and yellow roses dotted all over it. She looked absolutely stunning and much younger than her thirty-five years and she was sure Ravi would appreciate her. Basking in the bliss of the possibility of a reunion, she didn't feel hungry at all and skipped her lunch. At 1p.m., after ensuring that the front door was locked, she hailed an auto and embarked on her supposedly romantic journey.

On reaching the appointed place, she looked expectantly for Ravi amidst the bustling crowd. Her face lighted up on seeing him, standing erect, tall and handsome near a kiosk, looking at his watch now and then and alternating it with scanning the faces of the passers-by in auto or taxi, or foot. She recognized him easily, his swarthy complexion, sharp features, probing eyes and tall frame. How wonderful it was that he was still so slim and hadn't the slightest paunch on his belly which she hated in men, and for which she despised her husband. She told the driver to stop and when she alighted after paying, Ravi's eyes fell on her and it was as if his whole physical being lighted up with an immense joy, a profound, unfathomable happiness charged his whole mind and soul, and in that moment he realized he had found his soulmate. Yes, the same beautiful face, smart figure, and loving eyes. He rushed forward, his face beaming with an unaldered joy, and clasped Sheela's outstretched hand.

"Don't you feel ecstatic, Sheela, my dear, meeting after so many years. I say, you haven't changed much, looking so fresh and lovely, even at this age." Sheela was overcome with a strange kind of feeling, a pure bliss mixed with wonder and tinged with shyness. Tears of joy sprang up in her eyes and she stared at Ravi awestruck and dumb. "C'mon Sheela, what's this? I don't want to see tears in your eyes today, even though I know these are tears of happiness. Look, I too feel so great and wonderful like you, but let's enjoy this feeling, this wonderful moment." All of a sudden, Sheela's shyness vanished. She had found her long-lost friend and she must rejoice in the moment. She smiled at him affectionately, her eyes looking into his. "I do feel wonderful, Ravi. It's so nice meeting you after so many years."

"Then come on. Let's have our lunch. I'm awfully hungry. I'm sure you haven't eaten too.". Then holding his hand, he pulled her jostling his way amidst the crowd. When their bodies touched, an electric charge like lightning coursed through their veins and Ravi felt fully aroused.

For Sheela, her whole body and soul tingled with joy at his touch, and she enjoyed a strange kind of vibration in her whole being and she wanted this new feeling to continue forever and never end. But there was the crowd and there were the people all around, and she looked up at Ravi and felt he too thought the same. He smiled at her meaningfully. But she didn't know what that meaning held. However, they walked into a restaurant, hand in hand and Ravi ordered for two cups of coffee, which would be followed by lunch.

A soft music was being played as they sat opposite each other, sipping coffee happily. A slight blush tinged Sheela's cheeks as she looked up at Ravi's serious face; just then, his eyes met hers and both of them broke into a soft merry laughter. It sounded like a stream of water dancing over the pebbles.

"Wow, you look great!" Ravi broke the silence between them. "I really didn't believe it was you; but when I observed the slight tilt of your head and quizzical look of yours, I could guess from afar that it could be none other than you. Really, my heart just topsy-turvied."

Sheela laughed again, showing her pearly white teeth. "Surely, you flatter me. Nobody says I am beautiful, not even my husband." There was a tinge of sadness in her voice. Just then the waiter brought their lunch thalis.

Ravi could sense her sorow and cheerfully stormed in, "come on Sheela, does any husband ever praises his wife! I never praise my wife, though of course, she doesn't deserve it."

Sheela smiled and said. "here we are two long-lost friends, meeting each other after a long period of almost twenty years, must we talk about our spouses?" "What did you say, my dear! Are we just long-lost friends, or something better, greater, and more wonderful than that? Something more romantic!" There was a shy, seductive twinkle in Ravi's eyes which she found very attractive. "And what should we talk about?" He looked straight into her eyes.

All of a suden, Sheela felt very shy and her fair cheeks reddened easily. She lowered her eyes and said haltingly, "we can talk about ourselves—say, the weather—or even politics."

"Very boring topics indeed!" Ravi wrinkled up his nose and nodded his headd in disapproval. "We should be talking about something romantic. But since you don't feel inclined to talk, let's do something." Ravi' face was a portrait of delight.

"Right!" Sheela agreed. "Let's take a walk down the pavement and go the the park over there."

"No!" Ravi said decisively. "Some acquaintances may see us there. I think we should go to a room in a hotel. And be with each other comfortably there without the sun or any person looking down on us."

Sheela looked at him with dismay. "Hotel! Whatever for ? We can easily sit here and enjoy some time together. no, no, I cannot go to a hotel. And pray, may I know, what are we going to do there?"

"Make love, of course." Ravi said quite casually.

Sheela inwardly liked the idea. But she feigned disapproval. "No, no, I can't be so call-girlish."

Ravi felt his temper rising. "O come on, Sheela, don't be such a hypocrite." And then he softened his voice. "We are in love, we have been in love right since childhood. Then what's the harm in consummating our love?"

"No, no, it's immoral." There was something ominous in her tone. "What if my husband comes to know of it? He'll kill me straightaway. You can't imagine how short -tempered and cruel he is." Sheela looked at him in despair, like a lost child looking up at someone to guide the way.

"Sheela, don't be frightened." Ravi assured her, stretching his hand across the table and holding hers. And then a little more strictly. "and don't mind my telling you that you've really become silly and stupid. Where is that so—o intelligent Sheela I had known? You said your husband will come to know How will your husband know? We won't be doing it in the open, will we?" Ravi slightly annoyed, raised up his voice.

"Be quiet, Ravi." Sheela calmed him down. "There are so many people around. Someone may overhear, and the beginning may become the end. Let's be very careful, darling. Besides, right now, today, I don't want to betray my husband. I'll just feel bad, and suffer from a guilty conscience." She smiled sweetly at him, tongue-in-cheek.

Ravi, however, couldn't read her. He told her exasperatedly. "Since when have you been nurturing such stupid illusions like immorality, sin and guilty conscience. All rubbish, my dear, all rubbish. I don't believe is such shit! We love each other, and we ought to express our love and enjoy it to the full. I don't see anything wrong in it."

Sheela laughed. "O Ravi, I was only joking. Its only that I'm afraid of my husband. If he gets even the slightest hint of our romance, he'll make life hell for me, and our joy will come to an end."

"Sheela, please please, for heaven's sake, stop uttering 'my husband, my husband'. I'm fed up of hearing about your husband." Ravi was really angry. "Now, tell me, why at all did you inflame this long-lost love when only its embers remained.?"

The waiter had just brought the bill,and she was about to fumble in her purse to bring out the money, when he held her hand. "No, I'll pay." He said She looked into his eyes and was so drawn by it, as though she was sinking deep, deep into the ocean to reach a new, newer world of love and light. Ravi paid the bill and they both walked out, their sides dashing against each other lightly as they hurried along the crowded pavement. By now, it was already four o' clock and the chill of the evening was hanging on the air. As their bodies met, a thrill coursed down Sheela's spine. She looked at him and smiled and he winked at her naughtily, yet his voice was throbbing with sincerity as he said "Don't you feel great, enjoying this secret love affair. We feel so young again."

They walked along, deliberately allowing their bodies to touch each other. A tinge of ecstasy engulfed Sheela, as the first showers of Ravi's love fell on her dry, parched body; and a wonderful feeling emanated from her whole being, and it seemed to her as though it spread to everyone around her, for wherever she looked, the world was smiling and joyous. She did not want this feeling to cease; rather it should continue, she thought. She could not fathom his thoughts, whether he still loved her or not, but when he looked at her and smiled, she felt reassured. Even amidst the noisy crowd, they could only hear the sounds of the silence and stillness of love, which was magnetic and drew them closer to each other. Like a brook sallying down the hills, they flowed towards the bus-stop, unmindful of the people that pebbled their way. Sheela wished time would stop and not fly like it did, for then she would clasp these wonderful moments within her grasp and never let it go. Impulsively, she looked at her watch and saw that it was already half-past four. "Gosh! Its already so late. I have to go. My son will reach home at five o'clock, and I have to be home before that. And there's the bus to catch too." She snatched away her hand from his clasp, and was just rushing ahead, when he caught her up from behind.

Ravi looked dissappointed. "can't you stay a little longer?"

She smiled at him even through her hastiness. "Ravi, don't be so impatient. One should not be so hasty in love, right? Anyway, I'll meet you exactly at 11a.m. tomorrow, same place."

"but Sheela, tomorrow at 11a.m., I'l be in a meeting at the bank. I think I'll be free by one o'clock in the afternoon. Well,same place and same time as today. Exactly at 2 o'clock."

Bidding Ravi goodbye, Sheela once again rushed to the bus-stop and boarded a tram. She was just on time to reach before her son." Mama, I'm very hungry. Please serve my food very quickly. I have to go to the park to play cricket. And after that my tuitions are there." He said, throwing down his bag. He loved to talk to his mama while gulping down his morsels, and today, he was in a particularly talkative mood, but Sheela wasn't listening. Now and then, her mind wandered to Ravi, and a smile played around her full and luscious lips as she remembered those thrilling moments she had spent with her dear, darling Ravi. She wanted to bask in the exciting memories of it and drink all the happiness that she could derive out of it, but the daily household chores had to be attended to. Besides, her son was a little prattler and needed her attention.

"Mama, give me a little more fish curry. I've been asking you several times, but you aren't listening. What are you thinking of, mama?"

"Thinking nothing, my dear! Here, take a big piece of fish. I've specially prepared the curry for you. I'm sure its very tasty today. Would you like a little more rice with it, my wealth." Sheela fussed over him, all her motherly love brimming to the surfae.

"Yes, mama, give. But my friends are telling me I'm growing fattter day by day. Anyway, mama, today I was reprimanded by the teacher."

"Why?"

"Neeta ate up all the six cream biscuits from my tiffin box, and I got angry and hit her. She complained to the teacher, and the teacher rebuked me. Its too bad, really." The nine year old prattler talked on and on but Sheela was unmindful. Thoughts of Ravi gave her a strange pleasure and she wanted to indulge in it more and more, but the household affairs had to be attended to, and it was time for the evening prayers. However, in her heats of hearts, she thanked God for uniting her with Ravi one again. He was a ray of hope in her dull,squalid life. One moment, she was enveloped by an illusion fo love and joy; the next moment, it was stripped open, and she felt strange reality facing her on all sides when her husband returned from the office, looking disgruntled. A spurt of a strange kind of pitiable love sprang up in her; he looked so helpless and vulnerable. Her heart went out to him She deliberated being extra nice to him. "What's the matter, dear? You look irritated and annoyed."

"It's nothing. I don't want to trouble you with my problems in the office. I'm not feeling well either. And don't disturb me." The last words seemed more a warning than a statement. She was always scared of him. Since she hadn't brought a fat dowry,her husband, his mother and his sisters always looked down on her. She felt she was an unpaid servant in their house, always at her husband's and in-laws' service. She could never fathom her husband's mind. What he exactly wanted from her and what expectations he had of her, she could never really know or understand, though she had tried very hard to know in the initial years of their marriage. How different was Ravi, so frank and open-hearted. One good thing about Ravi was that he had no illusions about what he really wanted from life, and he knew how to express it well; and he compelled others to understand what he wanted. Sheela felt the moderns lacked this quality for which very often there was miscommunication. Her husband never even demanded sex from her as a matter of right, always cold and impassioned. In the early years of their marriage, it was she who always tried to arouse his sexual passion; but he never gave in to her; and if at all he made love, it was always perfuntory and as a matter of duty. Almost twelve years had flown by since then, and now her passion for him had cooled down. Looking at him as he supped his high tea, she felt he was just a piece of log, so dry and lifeless. How different Ravi was! She dreamt of the wonderful time she would have tomorrow from 2 p.m onwards to 5p.m. Her face shone with a peculiar glow, a flush which deepened into a blush as she imagined the wonderful way he would make love to her. How lucky his wife was! She envied her and was jealous of her.

5

Sheela woke up the next day as though a new dawn had opened up for her. She felt very excited and finished up her household chores with a speed which she had never imagined would be possible. How wonderful! Today, Ravi would make love to her! While they were in their teens, they had discovered their love, but they never had the time to explore it. His parents had passed away, and his uncle had come and taken him away along with his sister. As the train had moved away from the station and then fled off, and she had stood on the platform waving at him, it seemed as though her soul had been torn apart. How cruel fate was! She had cried and cursed her destiny then. Now, she thought, was the time to make up for all her lost pleasures. God had snatched her away from Ravi, but now he had brought them together again. She decided she would make most of her time with him. Today, come what may, she wouldn't spoil her mood or dread her husband's fastidious nature. He always found fault with her cooking, but as time passed, she had learnt to become indifferent to her husband's rebukes and criticisms and she always bore it with a stoic quietness. And today, she wouldn't mind it at all. Her mind wandered to Ravi now and then as she did her household chores, and when her husband left exactly at 10 a.m, she heaved a sigh of relief and slumped on the sofa to enjoy the feeling of being relaxed. Then she went to have a quick shower once again(for she had already had a bath on waking up in the morning), shampooed her hair, then adorned herself with a beautiful sari and imitation jewellery, sprayed on herself a beautiful body deo, and then hurried out.

The tram was overcrowded, but today she didn't feel the discomfort. She was oblivious of everything, except the fact that she was to meet Ravi. When she alighted at the bus-stop, her eyes fell on Ravi's anxious face as he searched for her amidst the crowd. His face lighted up on seeing her. In fact, it was a glow of delight. "come along, let's go to a hotel". He said, pulling her along.

"Hotel! Whatever for!" Sheela deliberately feigned surprise, so that she would get the full pleasure of Ravi persuading her gradually and then convincing her. But she realized he was in no mood to play about and wanted to rush to enjoy the bliss of love-making. "Come on, Sheela, don't be a hypocrite, darling; as if you don't know. Sheela, don't pretend. You know, I hate pretensions."

Sheela smiled sweetly. "Can't we have snacks first.?"

"We'll have snacks later. First, let's make love." He winked at her and smiled.

Sheela looked at him, wide-eyed, totally abashed . . . . How could he be so shame-faced to declare it so bluntly. Before she could utter another word, he pulled her along, and she sailed along with him, happy and joyous, like a fledgling who has just opened her wings. She would see and enjoy the whole, wide world of love, fresh, anew; and he was there beside her to help her in exploring the wonderful world of love. Ravi, on the other hand, felt that he had found his soul-mate and his life's ambition had been fulfilled; He gazed at her sweet, cute face, and buxom physique, and felt a surge of passion coursing through his blood. He would find his soul's fulfilment in her, he knew.

They went to a three-star hotel and booked a room for five hours. "But you'll have to pay the rent of a whole day." The receptionist said. "Anyway, in whose name shall I book?"

"Mr S. Das." Ravi lied.

"I want your proper and full name," the receptionist demanded.

"Mr. Soumya Ranjan Das," Ravi signed a false name. Sheela walked into room no. 32 of hotel 'Happy Smiles' and Ravi followed suit and bolted the door from within. Sheela wanted to look out from the window from the fourth floor, and she was walking towards it, but Ravi moved towards her with arms outstretched, held her by the shoulders and turned her around, drew her to himself and locked her in a tight embrace. "Sheela!" It was a caress. Then he kissed her lips and cheeks softly. "My sweet, my darling," he poured sweet endearments into her ears. "I had always dreamt of this, but had never imagined it would be possible. Really, your body is so soft.

Wow! I'm just melting into it." Sheela was in his arms, fighting to hold back the tears of great joy and at the same time finding it difficult to breathe. Nevertheless, her soul sang—"I'm home. This is where I belong." A warm, blessed feeling of peace engulfed her. Her half-broken heart was healed and she felt complete and a glowing within her as she held him. This is all that matters, she thought. And then her lips were on his, and they were in bed. They lay close together on the bed and gazed into each others' eyes and Sheela said, "love me" and Ravi experienced a beautiful feeling that had never happened to him before. He felt as though his body was on fire, and then he made a wild, passionate love, an ecstatic flight, which made the lovers soar higher and higher, deeper and deeper, and at last, they reached the seventh heaven of awesome delight. Several times they went through the journey, diving deep down and then soaring up higher and higher into the great depths of heaven. It was sheer bliss, a lovely journey; an amazing discovery, and then an exploration, and then again a discovery of something new each time they made an exploration. It was without a beginning or an ending, a river that swept Ravi along faster and faster, and the tide began to pull at him, drowning him deeper and deeper and then driving him higher and higher into a golden light, and then into a silky darkness that bombed into a million stars. And the wonder of wonders was that it happened again, and once again, until they lay there, breathless and tired. They needed a little rest, for they were totally spent out. Then they lay on the bed backwards, their arms stretched out,their legs dangling, and they themselves looking up at the ceiling. "Wonderful, wasn't it, my darling?"

"Superb!" Sheela agreed, and they both burst out laughing. "Well, I must be going." She said. **Two hours had flown past as one moment. At last, Sheela remembered that her son who might have come home from school, might be worrying about her. "O Ravi, will you love me always?" she asked. "Always, sweet Sheela, always." He replied**.

Ravi now felt himself to be a better person. All the pleasures of this beautiful world with all their glitter and dazzle seemed shabby to him compared with the pure joy he derived from the ardent friendship of this innocent soul. Their eyes met and Ravi could glimpse something of her pure soul reflected in her eyes. But Sheela was in a hurry to go. She looked at her watch. "Gosh! It's already half-past four. I have to be home by six o' clock." Hurriedly, she put on her sari and he his dress.

"I wish you could stay a little longer, my dear." Ravi said. "Anyway, come tomorrow, and let it be exactly like today. Meet me at the same place, same time. My train is at 6 p.m. From here, I'll straightaway go to the station."

"Okay, I'll come." she replied and hurried along the corridors of the hotel till she reached outside.

"Sheela, wait; I'll see you off". Ravi called out from behind. But Sheela didn't hear. Her mind was nagged by thoughts of reaching home. She hurriedly walked off to the nearest bus-stoppage.

"Mama, where had you been?" Her son petulantly demanded an explanation when she reached home. He looked sullen and angry. "I've been waiting at the dining-table for God knows how long; and you away somewhere. Anyway, I'm feeling terribly hungry. Quickly, give me some rice and curry. I have my tuitions." Sheela was fuming inwardly. Couldn't she have a day out even for herself. Wherever and whenever she went out, the idea of duty at home never allowed her a free space in her mind. However, she decided it wouldn't be wise to vent out her frustration on her son. Quietly and quickly, she went in and changing her sari, she slipped into a homewear. In a bid to deliberately subdue her ire, she was extra nice to her son and cajoled him gently. "Darling, my wealth, there was lunch in the kitchen; couldn't you serve it yourself. You're quite grown up, you know." Her son's mood had softened. "My dear mama, I know I'm grown up. But I won't behave like one." He smiled mischievously at her. Sheela knew it was no use arguing with him. She had spoilt him a bit. Anyway, hers was a routine life and just after her son had gulped his lunch and run for his tuitions, her husband sauntered in. He looked pale and sick, and she rushed forward to pull out this bag from his hands like an obedient slave.

Her husband allowed himself to be pampered. He derived a vicarious pleasure out of it, by belittling her, by making her think she was good-for-nothing, by making her feel inferior for she earned nothing. But she never felt inferior. She knew she was doing a hard job as a homemaker, looking after the home and the family. However, she behaved as though she was indeed inferior, only to satisfy him, only to keep him happy, and to avoid bickerings and quarrels, which inevitably ended up in being beaten by him. In the initial years of her marriage, such an attitude of her husband's had left her feeling crushed and frustrated, but as time passed, she had become used to such humiliation. And now she had accepted it as her destiny. But from now onwards, she would no longer allow herself to suffer. There was Ravi and just imagining him and knowing he was there for her worked like magic. It made her escape into a world of happiness, beauty and love. And she would make that much or little of joy dissolve into her sea of misery and make her life sweet, oh, ever so sweet. Enveloped in this feeling of sweet joy, Sheela hurried in to bring his tea and biscuit, and kept it on the table.

"Why do you have to give me biscuits every day? Can't you prepare some snacks just before I return home, say for instance, pakoras or samosas. You really are a good-for-nothing lady." He looked disgruntled. Sheela remained quiet as usual She didn't protest, for she knew it would fall on deaf ears. How could she convince him that the money he gave her for household expenses was too less and that she managed to make both ends meet with great difficulty? He was a man who was always dissatisfied, who seemed to worry too much unnecessarily, and always found a sadistic pleasure in belittling her because she hadn't brought a lumpsome dowry. How different was Ravi, really! So cheerful always, so carefree, seemingly without a care in the world. "Why should I worry?" He would say even when he was so young. ""Life is too short to worry about anything. One moment goes away and it means that our life is getting shorter and shorter. Everything is so temporary, so impermanent, and I don't want to waste my time bothering about such stupid and silly matters like the daily events in life. Its enough that I have life, and I am conscious of it and I want to enjoy life to the full whenever I get an opportunity. That's all." Looking back, she realized he was some sort of an existentialist, but albeit,with a difference, for he had in him a humane touch. Anyway, today, she didn't want her husband's taunts to spoil her mood. Her thoughts were full of Ravi, and she was jubilant. The springs of love which had almost dried up in her started oozing. She wanted it to gush out continuously, and flow along merrily, to God knows where, no matter what the destination. She had at last experienced the bliss of being loved and enjoyed the pleasure of love-making and she was looking forward to meeting Ravi again and indulge in such love adventures.

That day,her husband retired to bed earlier than usual. "What's for dinner?" He had asked.

"As usual, chappati and a veg curry." She had said quite casually.

"Anyway, I won't eat, for I am not feeling well."

"Are you having fever?" She had touched his forehead lightly and felt that the temperature was quite normal.

"No, not fever, but I'm having a terrible headache." Saying this, he had changed into his nightdress and gone to sleep. She slept beside him throughout the night; but they were strangers, not knowing each other at all, not even trying to know the hearts of each other, flowing along in the journey of life like two parallel boats. Initially, in the first few years of their marriage, they had made love to each other and a boy had been born. The darkness continued and continued. Sheela had tried to fill up the gap between them, by attempting to come closer, by trying to understand him, by adhering to all his wishes, by doing exactly as he wanted. But her husband never seemed to be satisfied and just remained indifferent. Over the years, the gap had widened, and now it had widened so much that they were strangers, unknown to each other, living under the same roof. Till now, the only silver lining, the ray of hope in her marital life had been her dear darling little son, Raja. But now, there was Ravi too.

6

After her husband had gone to the office the next day, Sheela, while cleaning the kitchen, hummed a soft tune to herself. She was as happy as a lark in the spring season, feeling like a fledgling who had just learnt to fly and was opening out its wings, with full of hope and desire for knowing the world. She had stepped into an enchanted, unchartered territory, the domain of love, and she dare not think of the future lest her present sense of adventure, boldness and joy, all combined together be spoiled. At half-past twelve, when she had finished up her chores, she washed and dressed herself well, sprayed on herself a sweet smelling perfume and put on her favourite saree. The joy of meeting Ravi was so overpowering that she felt exultant. Just then, the doorbell rang and Sheela was startled. "Who can it be?" she thought. "The milkman has already given the milk and gone. Must be the postman. Probably there's a letter for me." She opened the door and was aghast to see her husband looking feverish and sick. The heavens seemed to fall on her. O no! She had been looking forward to this meeting so much. And now all her plans were foiled

"What's the matter? You are a bit dissappointed on seeing me and don't seem very much pleased. I suppose you were going out. So well dressed up too! May I know where you were going?" he eyed her suspiciously.

Always suspicious, thought Sheela. Perhaps it was this suspicious nature that drove her to Ravi; this dearth of love and affection which every wife expects from her husband, which she deserved and didn't get and which she yearned from Ravi. Without waiting for an answer, he brushed her aside and went in. "Come over to the bedroom and massage my legs. Legs are aching terribly."

Sheela nodded her head in acquiescience. "I'll just clear the table and go." Her mind wandered to Ravi. He must have reached the rendezvous and must be anxiously waiting for her. How many times he would have anxiously looked at his watch. He is wondering why I didn't turn up, I'm sure, Sheela thought. She had his cell no. and thought of informing him, but how could she? The bloody landphone was in the bedroom itself! Anyway, appearing quite unmoved, she coolly went to the bedroom to abide by her husband's wishes when the phone started ringing.

"O some nuisance is calling! This phone irritates me. Do respond to the call, Sheela."

"Hello!" Sheela's voice was inaudible as she hissed out into the phone.

"Sheela!" it was Ravi at the other end and he was furious. "You still at home! What's the point in promising me and then betraying me at the last moment. It means you really don't love me."

Sheela held the receiver tightly to her ears, so that there was no space for any of Ravi's words to flow into her husband's ears. She cast a sidelong look at her husband. He was looking intently at her. "Dolly, I can't go with you, my dear. My husband has just come home from office. He's having fever. And I just can't go."

"What's this Dolly business, heh?" Ravi retorted back.

"please try to understand. I'll give you company some other day." And she abruptly put down the receiver.

"What was Dolly telling you?" her husband demanded to know.

Sheela felt nervous. Nevertheless, she replied boldly. "She had called me up a bit earlier, requesting me to go with her for she had some shopping to do. I had also agreed, and therefore I had dressed up. But now I don' t feel like going, what with you so sick."

"Anyway, let me sleep. Just massage my legs a bit."

While massaging, Sheela inwardly cursed her destiny, for depriving her of enjoying such lovely moments, moments full of love and sex. A delightful joy suffused her as she thought of Ravi's masterly, lustrous strokes, and she wanted to bask in the luxury of such thoughts, but that was not to be. Meanwhile, her husband's fever mounted; he became restless and demanded her attention more and more. "Bring me another cup of hot tea." He ordered.

But Sheela was feeling tired. "So much tea is not good for you. Particularly when you are having fever." She said wryly.

"Will you please shut up," her husband retorted. "Always advising me what to do or not to do. Just shut up your gab and do as you are told." Sheela had no other option,but to obey. She watched him intently,sipping his tea and enjoying every bit of it. She envied his power over her and his freedom too.

"Have you never seen me? Why are you staring at me like that?" How could he fathom what she thought about him? She, who never liked him, rather hated him. But feigned as though she was grateful to him for her bread and butter. ""Will you please massage my legs" he requested as he lay down to sleep. "my legs are aching." But it was more of a command. Somehow, she always felt scared of him and she could not say 'no' though she was extremely exhausted. The excitement of imagining being with Ravi and the successive disappointment of unfulfilment had drained away all her energy and had left her mentally and physically tired. As she massaged, she started yawning; even then, thoughts didn't vacate her subconscious. The springs of sexual urge had dried up within her husband. He never made advances, he never approached her for intercourse. The joy of being seduced was unknown to her ever since she had got married at the age of twenty-three. Prior to that, when she was just beginning to know the joy of being in love at the age of fourteen, Ravi's parents had been killed in an accident, and his uncle had taken him and his sister to Kerala. She pressed her hands mechanically on his legs, but thoughts of Ravi pervaded her whole being. She felt thrilled dwelling on him in the innermost recesses of her mind. She dare not make it obvious, lest her husband come to know and cut off her thread of enjoyment. Down, down the memory lane she drifted away. When she had waved tearfully as the train had moved away, it seemed as though her soul had been torn apart. How cruel fate was ! She had cursed her destiny then. Now was the time to make up for the suffering and pain she had felt. How many tears she had shed then. But now, she would not allow herself, or rather her mind to indulge in sorrowful thoughts or feelings. Ravi's handsome face flitted across her face and a smile tweaked at her lips. But at the same time, an uncertainty about her fate where love was concerned lurked in her. Did she have any power to make her love life blossom? After all, what was she? Just an unpaid servant in her husband's house. All talk of women empoweerment was sham. Her husband snored, and with a sigh, she rose and went to the kitchen and made a cup of tea for herself.

Some more days passed away, and all these nights, Sheela couldn't sleep well. Did Ravi, angered, make a detour and wouldn't advance further in their love-relationship? No, no, Ravi wasn't so immature, and therefore such doubts were unfounded. He truly loved her and was more a friend and confidante than anything else. She rang him up one fine morning at half-past eleven. Her husband was at the office and her son had gone to the school. "Is that Mr Ravi speaking?"

"hey Sheela, its me, your Ravi. By the way, since when did I become Mr Ravi to you? My God, you really ditched me that day. I waited and waited at the stoppage for two hours and then rushed to the station. Thank God, I didn't miss the train. But I'm not angry with you. I guessed you were caught up in a mess. I did feel inclined to ring you up all these days, but I withheld, lest you would fall into trouble again. Anyway, how are you?"

"I'm okay. That day I was just about to leave home to meet you, when unexpectedly my husband dropped in with a burning fever and heavy cold. Naturally, I had to stay back and take care of him. You know how suspicious he is. I lied to him that it was my friend Dolly who had called me up. Well, when are we meeting again? Really, forgive me for having kept you waiting."

"Sheela darling, please, no formalities between us. However, how did I know that your husband is such an irritating personality? Have I ever met him? Why don'tyou introduce me to him?"

"Ravi, this is not the time for joking. My telephone bill is rising and my husband may get suspicious again. Tell me when are we meeting again? Please arrange a rendezvous as quickly as possible." There was an urgency and anxiety in her voice which matched his desire for her too.

"Okay, I'm a bit busy with my office work right now. I'll arrange and let you know over the phone where and when, my dear."

"No, no, for heaven's sake, don'r ring me up. My husband may be at home amd may create a storm. I'll ring you up after a couple of days. Bye, love." She kept the receiver lightly, trying to savour the feel of his masculine voice for some more time which seemed to her as if it lingered in the receiver.

Her husband complained on returning from the office. "Sheela, I kept on ringing from the office several times at half-past eleven, but the phone was engaged. Why do you have to talk so much over the phone? The bill keeps rising and you know I'm not so rich."

"I didn't make a call. Lily rang me up." She lied, and she hated herself for it. She never used to tell lies before, but now circumstances were forcing her. "Anyway, why did you ring me up?" She wanted to know.

"A colleague of mine hadn't brought his lunch pack, and he is a diabetic; so I thought, well, if you could prepare a quick lunch for us, we could have eaten at home. Never mind, we had a wonderul meal in a new restaurant near our office. You'd have been put into unnecessary trouble."

Sheela looked at his flabby body as he went in to change into a homewear. He was a real glutton. No wonder he had grown fat and obese. Of late, he had developed a paunch; but she dare not tell him so, lest he rebuke her. As she looked at him closely, she imagined he looked like an ape, with his stooping shoulders and bulging belly. Already he was suffering from diabetes and hypertension, and at times, she felt it was her duty to advise him to control his diet, but she was scared of his fits of temper.

7

After almost a fortnight, Sheela rang up to Ravi. "hello Ravi, did you arrange a rendezvous?"

"Gosh Sheela! I've really forgotten. What with loads of work in the office, and problems at home too, it just slipped out of my memory." He was on tour to a small branch office in a nearby village and was having tea with a colleague.

"Really Ravi, how forgetful you can be; particularly in this matter, when you know there'someone who's dying to meet you and hear from you too"

"Sheela, I'll talk to you later." And he switched off. His colleague was looking at him intently and he didn't want to raise a suspiion. Sheela was sure that Ravi would call up after some time. It was a hot, sultry late morning, some half an hour before noon, and after tidying up the kitchen, Sheela went to have a bath. Trng—trng—the phone rang. Hurriedly, Sheela wrapped up herself in a towel and rushed out from the bathroom to the bedroom and picked up the receiver. "My dear, I'm so sorry I couldn't talk to you then. Now tell me what you have to say."

"I have lots and lots to tell you, but you don't have the time to hear, though,of course, I have the time to talk. I just want to tell you to quickly arrange for our next meeting."

"Okay, Madam" Ravi laughed. "by the way, why don't you come over to Mumbai?"

"You know that's impossible on my part."

"Why impossible? Ladies are being pilots, exploring space, and doing what not, and you say coming to Mumbai is impossible. Really Sheela, you're being too old-fashioned. Why should you be so scared of your husband? Just tell him you want to meet a friend."

"I'm sure you don't believe it is as easy as that, and you'r just pulling my leg. My husband's way of thinking is totally different from yours, and he is a very conservative type. You think only I am afraid of my husband and society; in fact, you are also scared of your wife and society too. You remember you switched off your phone a little while ago! I can very well guess why you did so. I'm sure your colleague was nearby."

Ravi laughed. "You've guessed right, my dear. However, I'v very little balance left. I leave it to you to decide where and when we shall meet, of course, at your convenience. You just name it, and I'll be there. By the way, write to me a wonderful letter overflowing with love and sweetness. Bye, I'm waiting for your letter. They are indeed pieces of literature."

How responsible and manly his voice was! It always seemed to mesmerize her and transport her to a beautiful world of love and romance. She knew it was an illusory world, but she impulsively clung on to the illusion. Though Ravi had switched off his cell, she held the receiver for some time to savour the feel of his voice. Putting down the receiver, she went into the bathroom and had a refreshing bath, all the while humming a soft, romantic Bollywood song to herself. She felt happy that Ravi had appreciated her letters. She put on a clean and washed set of clothes, and after performing a few rituals of daily prayer, she sat down to write to him.

Dearest Ravi, my soulmate,

How strange it seems now dear, that I could live, just live, though not happily, without having been in touch with you. I could not understand it then— just an 'emptiness within me, but now I know that l life without you was not life at all—just sadness and dreariness. Now when I don't see your eyes, the Bright moon turns dark, when I don't hear your voice the nightingale's song sounds dull, when I don't feel your breath, the gentle breeze annoys me. Why is it that the course of true love never runs smooth? Now, even in this 21st century, when the world has reached the peak of civilization, when live-in relationships is just

creeping into acceptance in our society, why, so why indeed, must we meet secretly, dreading exposure. It's very unfair that we have to always live in fear, unable to express and enjoy our love with absolute freedom. I think it's not so much as we are scared of society, but because we don't want to break off our family ties, our filial bonds. Isn't it absurd.! We love eah other, but we annot be together and enjoy this divinity and bliss. Tell me, my dear, did you suffer from a guilty conscience while making love to me? To be frank, I did feel a bit initially; guilty of infidelity, of breaking those marriage vows. But then I rationalized—why should I deprive myself of a little enjoyment which belongs to me? If I can find a little rosy happiness amidst this thorny gloom without causing pain to anyone and without harming anyone, it's only right that I should. After all, I think I'm a dutiful wife and daughter-in-law, and have always tried and am still trying to please my husband in every possible way. I love my son tremendously and have never neglected him. So what's the harm if I can extract. rather snatch away some moments of happiness which rightfully belongs to me, from my destined life?. Anyway darling, I'm boring you with my thoughts. Its time I should excite you—or should I say sexcite—you with my feelings. Do you remember that day when we were united in the hotel room? I had never imagined that there could be such a wonderful joy, so exquisite and beautiful in the union of our bodies and souls. I had read of such a joy in story books, but didn't know it would happen to me; me, amongst many whom fate had chosen to experience true love. it was a fantastic coming together, simply breathtaking and fabulous! I was deliriously happy, and felt as though the room and the whole universe was rocking and jazzing. And when you entered me, I felt something had exploded within me—an unbelievably marvelous journey, a coming and a departing, a beginning and an ending. It seemed to me as though the whole world had opened up to me with its infinite possibilities, and I was just floating in space, experiencing and enjoying in a single moment all that was there in the universe. Thanks for telling me to write to you; else I could never have told you my experience so shamelessly. To be frank, I'm crazy to enjoy this joy more, so please ring me up and tell me when are we meeting again. And remember, ring me up exactly between 11a.m—1p.m. I don't want to bore you further, so goodbye, my darling,

Love,
Sheela.

8

A fortnight later, at half past twelve in the afternoon, the telephone rang. Sheela picked up the receiver. "hello!" she said nervously.

"Hello, my dear!" Sheela knew it was Ravi. "Your letter was wonderful. It transported me to a beautiful world. Just now, I imagine you in my arms, and wow, it is a lovely feeling. Anyway, what are you doing right now?"

"Right now, I'm talking to you over the phone, stupid." Sheela giggled. "Thanks for insisting that I should write to you. I would have felt shy to tell you my feelings. Anyway, have you decided about our next rendezvous?"

"Yes. I'll be going to Bhubaneswar on some office work by the middle of next month, say from 14th-17th, I'm think aunty and uncle, I mean your parents are staying at Bhubaneswar. You've got a month's time to think of how you'll come to BBSR. And mind you, this time if you fail, you'll see what I'll do to you."

"I won't fail. I'll try my best to mollify my husband. By the way, you remember Ramesh! He's in the IAS. What a dull student he was. See, how luck favored him." Sheela was in a conversant mood.

"I remember everything, darling. How can I ever forget? Those long lazy summer afternoons, when we used to sit on the first floor of your half-built house, and sing hindi film songs at the top of our voices while the carpenters sawed the wood to make the doors and windows of your house. I think we had just entered into teenage then. These days, children are just incapable of enjoying such sweet innocent pleasures"

"Yes, they are so much obssessed with television and video games that there's no space in their mind for imagination."

"Well, you remember Ramesh's sister, Jayanti! O my God, what a greedy creature she was! You remember how in those hot summer afternoons, when your mother was busy sleeping, we used to shout to the ice-cream vendor, calling him to our door, that girl Jayanti used to come running to our house on some pretext ot the other and say ever so sweetly—Sheela, my father wants to read today's English paper, please give. And then we would offer her an ice-cream and she would greedily lap it up. Really, such childish imagination and innocence is missing in our children"

"Indeed, those were the good old days when there was so much passion for anything and something. Ravi, I've talked with you for a long time. I think I'm being a bit expensive for you. Last time you paid the entire hotel bill. And now your mobile recharge expenses are rising too."

"My dear, don't you think you have a right to my pocket. You are my friend and beloved, and can't I spend a bit for a very special friend whom I love tremendously. I spend two-third of my salary on my wife and son. Isn't it right that I should spend for tyou too. After all, you are the most valuable person in my life. O yes, I've just remembered, I have a new mobile set which I can gift to you so that we can talk for hours together."

"For heavens' sake, don't do that, Ravi. It'll give rise to unnecessary complicacies. And you don't know my husband. He'll kill me straightaway if he to know of our affair."

"But how will he know? Certainly, you'll take care to keep it a secret. And I'll also recharge your cell from time to time".

"I don't need the cell at all. I'll ring you up from the landline at times, whenever possible. However, forget it. I'm sure you have a lot of work which is pending. I promise you I'll try my best to go to BBSR. Bye, thanks for calling."

"Bye, Sheela. I'm waiting for the day when I can again hold you in my arms. Here's a flying kiss for you." And then,he switched off. Sheela kept down the receiver and smiled. Really, how childish he was.

That night, Sheela snuggled up to her husband, but he pushed her away. "I want to sleep. Don't disturb me. I'm tired." He grumbled.

Sheela pretended to be hurt and angry. Undoubtedly, she was scared of her husband, but she spoke up. "Don't I have a right to demand love and affection from you? After all I'm your wife. I don't know why you are so indifferent towards me! Have I ever hurt you? Have I done against your wishes?"

"O please shut up! Don't jabber near my ears. I want to sleep." Fear rose up in Sheela, but she remained undaunted. She felt like stabbing him, but feigning as though her pride had been hurt, she continued. "Tell me, why do you behave with me in this manner? If you think I'm unworthy of you, leave me in my father's house for some days and see if you can manage without me? I haven'g gone home for almost six months, and Papa rang me up calling me home." And she started crying.

"Okay, don't cry. But why do you want to go to your house at this time of the year? Who will manage here? Besides, Raja's school is there. He can't afford to miss his studies and go with you, cn he?"

"He won't be missing schol at all. Next month, 14th and 15th are holidays, and including Saturday and Sunday, it means a four-day package. Please dear, let me go." Sheela pleaded. "I haven't seen Papa and Mama for so long. You can have your meals in the office canteen. Its only a matter of four days."

"Okay, if you insist, you may go. But ther's still one month's time. Its too early to decide." He started yawning.

Sheela felt happy. "Will you mind if I request something of you tonight?" her tone softened. "We haven't fucked for so many days. I really want to do it today." And she hugged him tightly.

"How shameless you are!" And he laughed sarcastically.

"Why shameless?" Engulfed in the feeling of love for Ravi had somehow emboldened her and gave her the courage to speak up. "Can't I demand this much from my husband! After all, we took an oath before the Gods that we would be one in body, mind and soul, So come on, please." She looked at him beseechingly with a sexual glint in her eyes, even the most indifferent and passionless heart would melt. But he just stared at her with a stony blankness for some time and then said "no, I'm not in the mood today. I'm too tired and don't disturb me further. I'm feeling sleepy. We'll have it some other time." He put away her hands and rolled over to the other side and began falling asleep.

Sheela heaved a sigh of relief. This playacting was getting on her nerves. But she had to mollify him. Thank God he had refused. Otherwise she would have to go through the most disgusting journey with him while her soul would be crying for companionship and union with Ravi. She felt glad and looked forward to her togetherness with Ravi.

9

Ravi rang up to her after a couple of days. It was half-past twelve in the aftenoon and Sheela instinctively knew it was Ravi. Between 12.30 and half-past one was the usual time during which he rang up. For he knew that her husband would be busy in his office during that time. And Sheela never went out on an errand or did marketing at that time. Even if she required some vegetables or grocery urgently, she would rather request the neighbour's servant and give him some cash-tips than go herself. As for ringing up to her friends or for door service at that particular hour, it was out of question, les Ravi tang up and her phone would be engaged. Everyday, she waited expectantly for Ravi's call. Very often, she was tempted to pick up the receiver and dial Ravi's cell number, but she daren't; lest her husband scan the telephone bill and may doubt that there's something wrong with the bill and make unnecessary enquiries. However,she knew it was an absurd idea but she thought she could distinguish Ravi's call from somebody else's. now, she knew it was Ravi's. She rushed to the phone and picked up the receiver. "Hello!" Ravi's voice was clear and distinct.

"It'me, Ravi, your Sheela!" and she laughed out of sheer relief. "Anyway, why weren't you ringing up all these days?"

"Well, I was a bit busy with a lot of bank work. You know banks; how they make you work so hard. You don't get a moment's respite, particularly when ou are promoted to a senior rand. Plus, I was trying to arrange a duty leave to Bhubaneswar all these days. You see, they were sending me to Hyderabad. Luckily, and very tactfully, I managed to make it to BBSR, and on those particular days too."

"Well, great! How did you manage it?" Shhela had some interest in knowing about bank work.

"You won't understand the intricacies, darling, so it no use explaining to you. However, I've fixed up the date from 14th to 17th. 14th is Thursday, and on that day and the 15th, I'll be having a bit of job work in the bank; and 16th and 17th being Saturday and Sunday respectively, we'll be having a heaven of a time. And don't disapppoit me any more. I won't take no for an answer or accept any excuse for that matter. It's your job how you'll convince your husband to grant four days' casual leave. By the way, have you applied for sanction of leave?"

"Ravi, how easily you can joke about it. But for me it's a helluva job." There was a sense of uncertainty in Sheela's voice.

"I'm sorry if I've hurt you. But forget it. I've talked with you for a long time. I wish I could talk with you for hours, but there's a lot of work to be done. Gosh! There's still a one-month before we can be together and then we'll talk and talk and in between make love too. And mind you, be very bold about it, without having any misgivings about commititng sin and all that rubbish. I want to relive those wonderful, glorious moments of the past." Sheela felt thrilled to hear his voice and allowed him to do all the talking and felt a curious pleasure as her mind travelled down memory lane. Just then, the doorbell rang. She literally jumped, thinking her husband may be at the door.

"Ravi, someone's at the door. I'm putting down the receiver." And she ran to open the door. She heaved a sigh of relief when she saw the milkman. "Why didn't you come in the morning?

"my son fell down from the bike and I had to take him to the hospital." The milkman said. Had it been some other day, Sheela would have pounded him with questions about how he fell and so on and so on. But just now, she still hadn't got off the euphoria of Ravi's call. And she wanted the euphoria to continue. She had great interest in knowing about other people's lives and she alwauys wanted to hear something new. Very often, she felt bored and disgusted with her loveless and lacklustre life. But she never wanted her life to fade into dullness and stupidity. She wantd to keep alive in herself the spirit of learning, pursuing knowledge to as much extent as possible. No dount fate hadn't given an opportunity, but she wantd to keep her mind vibrant and active. She believed in the maxim that as long as you learn, you remain active and young. She had a burning intensity to learn something new everyday; but how could she? If she wanted to learn music or singing, money was required, and her husband never gave her any 'extra money'. After tolerating his whims and fancies for some years, she was gradually getting fed up of his ways, and now she become indifferent to his feelings, and accepted her stoically, shifting, her interest to other avenues Just then Ravi had come into her life like a breath of fresh air, like a whiff sweet fragrance. She didn't want to spoil her mood by thinking of husband's miserliness. Somehow, thoughts of ravi invaded her mind every now and then and it became increasingly difficult for her to fight it away and concentrate on her work. Rather, she found great pleasure and satisfaction in indulging in thoughts about Ravi. Love is indeed a great power, she realized. Since she was always happy now, assured that someone isalways there whom she truly loved and who loved her too, she became more patient and tolerant and everready to do what her husband or son ordered. Of late, her husband had mellowed too. Probably, she had realized her worth. Now, when she no longer wanted any affection from him, he was beginning to treat her well. She did not want it to be so, lest she felt guilty betraying him. But was she really betraying him? Of course not! She had every right to enjoy love, life and friendship when God himself or fate herself was ofering it to her. Why indeed should she deprive herself form enjoyment. Thus she justified herself and always basked in thoughts about Ravi. Life had definitely acquired a new meaning for her.

Throughout the month, she kept on coaxing, persuading her husband to allow her to go to her parents' place, and he never said no. Meanwhile, every alternate day, Ravi kept on ringing to know about her progress in her plans to come to BBSR. She loved to listen to Ravi, his problems in the bamk, his son's smartness, etc, while her son was overjoyed at the prospect of visiting his grandparents, and enjoy some days of their pampering. During breakfast one Sunday, when Raja heard his parents talking about her visit to her parents, he intervened. "Papa, let us go. It'll be great fun. And grandpa keeps inviting me always. When are you coming, hero, he tells me over the phone."

"But you'll miss school. Besides, you'll lag behing in your studies, too. And the most important fact is that I will miss you." His father smilingly told him.

"But Papa, Saturday and Sunday are holidays, thus I'll be missing school only for two days. Some of my friends stay away for a month when they are sick or when there is a function in their house. So two days absence will not hamper my studies at all. Besides, I'll take my books and homework copies too. As for missing me, you won't;' cause you'll be busy in your ofice work. Besides, just think of my grandparents! They love me so much and want me to be near them for some days. How can I disappoint them? So let us go. Papa, please." The little prattler looked so beseechingly at his father, that he didn't have the heart to say no.

"Okay, both you and your mother will go, but on Monday, you must come back and be here,at home, by evening, right?"

Sheela remained quiet, feigning indifference, as though it was an unimportant matter for her. But in her heart of hearts, she delt great joy. Her heart felt happy as a lark in Spring, for she would be near her dear dear Ravi for some days. But she was careful and clever enough not to express her happiness eloquently on her face.

10

The great day came when sheela and her son boarded the train to BBSR. Six months had passed since she had gone to her parents house, and now she was feeling glad that she would have a few days rest from dull, boring household chores. Her mother always sympathised with her when she came home. "You work so hard there; here, you take rest. We'll look after Raja too." And then, there was Ravi this time, with whom she would spend some time, and perhaps make love too. O, it was so exciting,an adventure, the mere thought of which thrilled her and made her tremble with joy.

The train sped past mountains, hills and dales. She loved to watch the scenery and after having lunch from the pantry, she and her son took a siestaa. On waking up, they found they had neared the BBsr station. They gathered the luggage near the door and waited for the train to halt. Her parents came rushing forward to help her alight and they kept on fondling Raja throughout the auto journey. A delicious meal of hot rice, dum aloo, fish curry, fried brinjal and chutney was awaiting his palate and just as she had finished eating, her father said. "Well, Sheela, I got my pension arrears, so I bought a Nokia mobile set for you. I've already put an airtel simcard in it. Your nimber is 9871256819." He brought it out from an old wooden almirah and gave it to her. "Now,you can ring me up whenever you like. When your balance finishes, I'll recharge it from here."

"O papa, thank you so much and so sweet of you. Surely I can recharge my phone." Sheela said, for she did not want o disclose to her parents that her husband never gave her enough to spend. Or any pocket money either. She felt happy because now she could ring up to Ravi whenever she liked.

"Mama, I'll be back within half-an-hour form Sujata's house" and sheela went off, leaving her parents to take care of Raja. Here, she felt light-hearted, relaxed, throwing off all caution and care to the wind and without any responsibility at all. Sujata was her friend in the neighbourhood and was working in an MNC and was still not married. Spinsterhood was her comfortable zone and she didn't want to exchange it for wifehood or motherhood. While walking to Sujata's house, she pressed Ravi's number in her cell. It was 70'clock in the evening and she thought ravi would be in hid office. "hello," Ravi's voice made Sheela's heart throb with joy.

"I'm at home." Ravi's voice was grave. Sheela guessed his wife was beside him. "Don't disturb me. I'm very tired." And he switched off. Ravi's wife grumbled. "Why do these office people have to ringup to you here also. Never leaving ou a moment's peace or a little time for your son. Olf! These ofice people. Our Som is having a terrible cold and I told you to bring some medicine, but you forgot." She nagged.

Ravi had really forgotten. While returning home from office, his thoughts were about Sheela and how much he would enjoy their togetherness. "okay, I'll consult the doctor and bring it just now." And he rushed off, fearing an altercation. It was always like this, she complaining and nagging, always dissatisfied, and he retorting furiously, ultimately ending in a violent quarrel. Therefore he shot off, not wanting to spoil his mood just now.

Sheela was busy gossipping with her friend when her cell rang. "Sheela, I don't have much time to talk toyou right now, but Tomorrow, I'm reaching BBSR at 9a.m. by flight. I'll be with you exactly at 1 o'clock in the afternoon. But tell me, where will you be waiting for me?"

"I'll think it over and tell you tomorrow after you reach here."

"No, no, let's decide now itself. Just wait a minute, yes, I've got it. I'll be waiting for you in the foyer of Sishmo hotel at Wellingdon Square. Reach exactly on time. I'll be waitng for you. I love you, Sheela." And Ravi switched off.

That night, Sheela couldn't sleep well. Pangs of guilt complex jabbed at her heart now and then, like a sword stabbing, and try as hard as she could to ward it off, nothing prevailed. Was she doing the right thing? Surely, it's a sin betraying one's husband! But then, her husband deserved to be betrayed. Not even once did he try to understand her or love her. She was just a servant who was being paid for her services with food, clothing and shelter. Her whole being revolted against this kind of living, but she had chosen to put on the garb of a good wife and mother, and now it was difficult to take it out. Thanks to Ravi, he was a bright light shining, and had brightened her drab and grey world. True, she felt a bit sorry for Ravi's wife,whom she felt she was deceiving; but then, as a human being, she too had every right ot enjoy her life and make the most of it. "What if my husband comes to know of my extra-marital relationship. He'll kill me. I'm sure." These thoughts tormented her throughout the night and then she fell asleep.

11

At the ring of her mobile at 9 a. m. in the morning. Ravi's voice boomed into her ears. "Sheela, I'v reached here just now. I have to be ready for the meeting. After the meeting, I'll rush to the hotel's foyer. You must be there by half-past twelve. Bye."

While she was having breakfast, her father said. "Sheela, it's good that you slept till so late. After all, you have so much work to do in your house. You hardly get proper sleep there. My advice is, take as much rest as possible while you are here, instead of roaming about here and there which will again make you tired."

"O dear Papa," Sheela held his hand affectionately. "I've come here afer six months, is it only to sleep? No Papa, I must meet my friends, roam about here and there, and enjoy myself thoroughly. O yes! Shibani has invited me to her house for lunch, so that we can relive our good old days." Generally, she avoided telling lies to her father, but in this case she couldn't help it. "papa, you must do me a favour. I don't want to take Raja with me. He'll disturb me like hell. He'll keep on saying—"let's go home, let's go home."" Just then, her mama came in. "Mama, please take care of Raja while I'm away for some hours. I'll come back in the evening."

Her father smiled, "Sheela,do you have to request this of us ! Of course we'll take of Raja. It'll be a great pleasure for us. We love his prattle and he is such a smart boy too. You go and enjoy yourself as much as possible."

Sheela heaved a sigh of relief. When she was just about to leave at 12 noon, her son said "mama, where are you going?"

"To a friend's house, my dear."

"I too want to go with you. Please,mama, take me along with you."

"No,my dear, it'll be very late by the time I return, and you'll feel hungry. Don't worry, your grandpa will give you a ride in the auto and take you to the park in the evening afer you wake up from your siesta." She kissed him gently on his cheeks.

"Okay," and his face brightened up.

Sheela shot out of the house, for she feared he may change his mind and insist on going with her. She reached the foyer of the hotel at 12.25p.m. and felt exultant. Her gaze kept riveting towards the gate, and exactly at 12.40, she saw a car halting in front. Her heart raced rapidly as she saw Ravi step out of the driver's seat. On seeing her, he waved and a smile lit up his handsome face. How smart and slim he looked as he walked down to her, she thought. He quickly took his hand in his and his gaze smiled at her. A slight blush lighted up her fair cheeks and suddenly she felt very shy. "So, Sheela, you're here at last! Let's go to a very quiet place. I must say you're looking very beautiful. And you've grown slimmer too since the last time I saw you."

"Ravi, you too look very handsome. No one will ever say you are thirty six years old. You look like a young man of twenty-five." And she laughed. She looked good and felt great as she walked beside him and she felt as though she was on cloud nine. Their bodies touched and she felt love emanating from the warmth of his body and pervading her whole being.

"Now, look here, my dear, we have some hours for ourselves. Have you planned what we shall do?." Ravi asked Sheela.

"O yes! We'll just talk and talk to our heart's content." All of Sheela's innocence and naivete came to the forefront when she was with Ravi.

"Only talk and nothing else?" Ravi raised his eyebrows and looked quizzically at her. Again the blood rushed up to her cheeks. "We'll think about that later. Let's get out of here first.". It was a busy market-place and she was just stepping into the car when she heard a voice behind. "Hello Sheela, it's you! My God, I hadn't seen you for so many years. How nice!" The woman then looked at Ravi. "Wow! Your husband looks quite young, my dear. Perfect match, I should say. Come along, both of you. Our house is nearby." And she pulled Sheela's hands. It was a post-graduate batch-mate of hers. Sheela looked at Ravi helplessly.

"Look here,madam." Ravi addressed the batch-mate. "We'll come some other day. I have some urgent work in the office and I have to drop her home. By the way, I'm not her husband. I'm just a friend of hers."

"O Sheela, I'm so sorry to have mistaken him for your husband. Anyway, come along, just a cup of tea and nothing else. My mom will be so pleased to see you." Her house was just a couple of yards away.

"Really Sheela, you still look so young and pretty. Not a trace of age in you. My Rita has grown plump." Her mom said. "Anyway, where's your son? Why didn't you bring him.?" She laid down two cups of tea and a plate of sweetmeats and samosas on the teapoy in front.

""Aunty, why did you take the trouble of making tea? Now its actually lunchtime, but since you've given, we'll drink it." Sheela said. "I am in a bit of a hurry. I'll come some other day." Just then, Rita's daughter came in and bowing down, touched their feet, as a gesture of 'pranam.'

"My granddaughter, Guddi, very intelligent, always busy with her studies, got 90% in her school finals." And the garrulous woman talked on and on. How the hell did we get stuck up here, thought Ravi and told Sheela

"finish your tea quickly. We have to go, Aunty. Thanks for yor tea,we really needed it." And Ravi did 'Pranam' and walked out, followed by Sheela.

"Oof! Thank god we dared to come out; if not she would have wasted our whole day." Sheela remained quiet as Ravi drove on. "I really can't understand why people ae so egoistic as to think that everybody would like to know about their children, themselves and their achievements. Why should we want to know about them at all?"

"Please, Ravi don't be so annoyed! You were so tolerant in school." Sheela laid her hands on his lap and tried to cool him down. She smiled at him. He laughed "Sheela,how can I be angry with you beside me! You, my sweet sweet darling."

"I'm sure you've said that to your wife several times."

"For heaven's sake, don't bring in my wife between us. She's a cantankeous woman with a tongue as sharp as a razor which pierces, cuts and brings out all the anger and frustration in me. When we are together, let's totally forget about her. Its our day and lets make the most of it". His tone was decisive.

"But Ravi, where are we heading to now?'

"We are going to Nampur. Its only 50kms from here. The beach is the most ideal spot or lovers where we can sit and talk for hours together, and also make love too."

"Let's reserve the second part for tomorrow." And she cast a sideway smiling glance at him which he found most attractive.

"I say, I'm terribly hungry, and before we go there,we must have a very good lunch. My stomach is yawning with hunger and I am sure yours is, too."

"Then let's go to Paradise Inn"

"yes indeed! Ater a sumptuous meal, we can proceed. I suppose you take non-veg on Fridays?" asked Ravi.

"No, I don't take on Fridays."

"But I do. In fact, I love to eat non-veg everyday. I don't believe in this humbug at all. Either you are a pure veg or a pure non-veg. This idea of eating fish on Wednesday and not eating on Saturday somehow doesn't make sense to me. Of course, I don't object to you obeying such rules." He smiled sweetly at her. "Anything you do is okay for me. You know why? Because I love you."

"Do you really love me?" Sheela asked deliberately because she loved to hear 'I love you' from Ravi

"I think I don't know." On seeing her face saddening a bit, he laughed and said. "But one thing I am certain about, I feel gorgeous when I think of you, when I imagine about you and when I am near you. All my sorrows, my tensions and problems just vanish into the air when you are beside me." And Ravi's face had a faraway look.

"Ravi, we've just crossed a restaurant" cried out Sheela. "Really, love has the power to make us hungry."

After ordering two meals,both of them just relaxed in their chairs. "Phew, it's hot. Thank God, it's an AC restaurant." Sheela said.

Suddenly there was a voice from behind. "Hello, Sheela, it's you! Wonder of wonders!" Sheela turned around to see her maternal aunt smiling at her. "O my dear, I'm seeing you after so many days." Her aunt continued. "I always ring up to your mom and enquire about you. She says you are fine. Not even once do you ring up to your aunt. Your husband hasn't come?" She looked around as if searching for Sheela's husband. "Why didn't you bring your son?" She attacked sheela with questions one after another without giving her a chance to answer. And it ended with a suspicious glance at Ravi." Anyway, who is he?"

"He is my school classmate. I had come here shopping and I met him. Both of us felt hungry and thought we could have lunch here.

"Lunch here? O no, I've cooked mutton today. I saw you from outside and came rushing to you. Dear me! I never had the opportunity to invite you after your marriage. Come along. Today I'm not going to leave you without having lunch. You must come." She looked quite stern. Ravi looked helplessly at Sheela, expecting her to save themselves from the situation. "But dear Aunty, I'll come some other day. You see, Ravi wouldn't like to eat anywhere else other than a hotel. Please try to understand."

"Why not? If I'm your aunt, I'm also his, since he's your classmate"

"But Aunty, I don't take non-veg on Friday." Sheela felt annoyed with her aunt, but she did not want to sound rude.

"I've cooked veg items also; now come along and don't fuss about too much. Or else I'll think you don't care for your aunt at because she is poor." Of all her nephews and nieces, aunty liked Sheela the most because of her friendliness and adaptability to any situation. As she led the way, Ravi chatted with Sheela. "You seem to be quite popular. Wherever we are going, people are inviting you for tea or lunch. Really, Sheela I'm proud of you." He shrugged his shoulders.

"Pleasse, Ravi, don't joke. It's absolutely irritating. Even dame luck is conspiring against us and not allowing us quality time together. "She winked at him.

After eating a delightful lunch cooked by Sheela's aunt, both of them drove down to Nampur, a seaside resort, about 40 kms away from BBSR. By then, it was almost half-past three, and Sheela had promised her father that she would be back by six o'clock in the evening. But she suppressed her worries lest Ravi's mood be spoilt. However, Ravi showed his displeasure at the crowd in the beach. "Let's go to a lonely area." Sheela agreed and smiled cheerfully at him, and they went to a far corner of the beach where a few boatmen were busy hauling their boats. A boatman advised "Sir, its dangerous out here. Big waves come all of a sudden and catch you off guard and drag you along with the current." Ravi didn't reply. He was intently looking at Sheela. Suddenly, he drew her close to him, and hugging her tightly, kissed her lips Time stood still for both of them as they were locked into eternity. And Sheela wished these beautiful moments would never pass away. After having had his fill of this beautiful experience, Ravi abruptly withdrew. "it was bliss, wasn't it,my dear."

Ravi looked deeply into her eyes. "Yes, it was wonderful." A soft smile lit up Sheela's beautiful face. And they stared at each other like two small, innocent children who have discovered something new. On looking around, they were aware that some boatmen were staring at them. Apparently enjoying a live love scene. Suddenly Sheela felt very shy and said, "Ravi, please lets get away from here."

"no, let's stay. Nobody recognizes us here. Somewhere else, we may come across some acquaintances and it may brew trouble."

Sheela saw wisdom in it. They sat down on the beach, huddled close together,holding each others' hands. The waves lapped gently at the shore as the lovers stared at the wide expanse of the sea enjoying the music of the ocean and the silence of each other. "Darling," Sheela broke the silence. "Don't we feel like Rose and Jack of 'the titanic'. Only, they were on the deck and we are on the beach." She turned her gaze towards Ravi and then put her head on his shoulders.

"Just look at the horizon where the sky meets the sea. You can't distinguish between the two, can you? The sky and the sea seem one. The waves are in the sea and the sea is within the waves. Similarly,we are in the universe and the universe is within us. How logical it is! I don't realize why people don't understand this." Sheela gazed at him, wide-eyed and marveled at his spirituality and it dawned on her that love is indeed a spiritual experience.

"why are you gaping at me like this, Sheela?" Ravi wa surprised.

"I was wondering how spiritual you are, and I admire you for it."

"I think it is quite simple, nothing very spiritual about it; here, the sun and the sand, the sea and the silence helped me to listen to the musical symphony of the waves. It helped me to meditate for a moment and realize the self in me. And with you beside me. I feel I no longer have any worry, problems or obstacles." He clasped her hands and wringing it excitedly, he cried out "O, I've discovered love—a wonderful, joyous feeling. It makes you absolutely fearless, for you've got the best thing in the world which nobody can snatch away from you. Its this blissful feeling of loving someone."

Just then, Sheela's cell rang. It was her father "Hello Sheela, where are you? I can hear the sound of waves dashing against the shore. O my God, have you gone to Nampur? Why did you go so far? Anyway, please don't go too near the water; it is dangerous."

"Papa, don't worry about me. I've come here with Anita. She and her friends were coming here on an outing, and when they told me to join them, I agreed."

"mama," her son called out. "how come you went without taking me. I would have enjoyed it a lot."

"Sorry, my dear. I'll bring you on some other day. Tell grandpa I'll be reaching within an hour. We are just starting on our return journey."

Sheela looked at her watch. It was already half-past five. The sun was setting but there was no time to feast on the beautiful scenery. "Let's go back." She said.

A tinge of annoyance clouded Ravi's face. "Even in this highly, tehnological modern age, where live-ins are also accepted, I can't understand why we two can't be together, as we wish. I wanted to spend the night with you in a good hotel, but that is not written in our fate. It's really exasperating."

Sheela smiled reassuringly at him. "Darling, I promise you tomorrow I'll fulfil your wish. But it won't be in the night, It'll be in the daytime. You see, we have to be very careful, If anyone comes to get even a hint of our relationship, it'll lead to many problems and may even be the end. Let's hope to enjoy our secret love as long as possible.

"Maybe you are right." Ravi seemed to get the point. "I don't want our idyllic joy and bliss to end forever. Let's go."

As Ravi drove along, they talked about their childhood days. "You remember how we got lost one early summer afternoon,when there had been no rain for days, while crossing the river bed, intending to visit our carpenter's house, but instead we landed up in a den of thieves. Thank God,your father's friend in that village guessed something was amiss and very tactfully, he got us out of the mess."

"Yes, and we were truly such an adventurous lot. Children these days are so different. They are always couched up watching tv, or doing computers, or perhaps busy with their studies. And parents too in those days trusted their children. They really believed that we would never do anthing that they would be ashamed of. Things are so different these days. Somehow that trust between children and parents is missing.

"Yeah! And that Raghav. Who'd imagine he would be an IAS officer'. Such a quiet, lousy fellow he was. Six months ago, I came across him in Bhopal, where I had gone on a tour. He recognized me immediately and proudly flaunted his IAS satus. MP cadre, I think. He invited me to his bunglow. Aunty was pleased to see me and talked about the good old days, her wonderful daughter-in-law, and the fat dowry Raghav had been gifted with. They were a greedy lot even at that time."

"And his sister Jayanti. God,what a glutton she was!" And both of them laughed. "You remember, when we would call the ice-cream or cake vendor, she would overhear it and come rushing to our house on some pretext or the other, so that we would give her a cake or an ice-cream."

"Really, what a sweet and innocent girl she was.! Such simplicity is lacking these days. Modern children know somuch about everything, thanks to TV and internet, that they've lost the sense of wonder. And Sheela, you too were so innocent and simple. Believing in all the lies that people said,with never a bad thought or an evil idea in yur mind. And I liked you for it; never a negative thought in your mind. So positive you were, really."

Again there was a call for her. It was her mother. "Sheela,where are you? Raja is crying and demanding to know why you aren't back."

"Ma, I'l be reaching within half-an-hour. Give him the phone. I'll explain to him."

"He's not at home. Your father took him out to buy a dairy milk chocolate."

"ma, don't give him so many chocolates. He's having a toothache."

"How else can we pacify him.? By the way, Your husband had rung up and I told him you had gone out."

"Okay, Ma, I'll reach soon. Don' worry." And she switched off. Just then, Ravi received a call.

"Hello! When are you returning to Mumbai?" Ravi's wife shrieked at the other end.

"I'll be returning on Sunday." Ravi retorted angrily. Sheela lay her hands on his lap and eyes suggested that he should calm down.

"But you said that you would return tomorrow. And Som is really not well. He complains of pain in his legs. If you come soon, we'll show him to a good doctor. Anyway, did you have your lunch on time? I hope you've had."

"I had a delicious lunch in somebody's house."

"Must be a bank officer's house, I'm sure." Ravi's wife didn't wait for an answer, but continued. "Come soon. I'm really missing you. I do love you so much,you know, and take care of your health. And also bring a nice handloom saree for me, please."

"Okay, a saree for you, and also a dress for Som. At present, I'm a bit busy, and I'll ring up to you later. Bye!" And he switched off.

Again the cell rang. Ravi looked at the number and annoyed, he asked "Now,what is it?"

"You said you were busy. But you are not in a meeting. You are on road, going by car, I suppose. I can hear the noises of lorries and buses moving past. Tell me, whose car is it?"

"You see, I'm driving and the car belongs to my friend And you know, how dangerous it is to talk on the cell while one is driving, and that too on the national highway."

"O, I'm really sorry, dear, for disturbing you. Your life is more precious to me than anything else in the world. But don't forget my saree." And she switched off.

"Your wife seems so sweet and affectionate. She loves you so much too. I'm really feeling jealous." Sheela looked at him and smiled.

"you need not feel jealous at all. For I do not love her. You are my first love and you'll remain so forever. "Ravi said decidively.

"I'm envious of her not because she is receiving your love but because she is capable of loving you so much, which I thought was exclusively my right" And Sheela looked sad

"capable of love, my foot!" Ravi retorted angrily. "She only loves the bucks which I give her at the end of each month. And she's 'terribly mean, too. None of my relatives like her. She doesn't even allow me to spend any money on them,when necessary. How selfish she is! I really don't like her."

"You shouldn't say such things. After all, she is your wife." Sheela argued.

"She yells and shouts at me like anything. When I first brought her to Mumbai to liive with me, you know what her first question to me was! How much is your salary? You must give everything to me. All my deams of a loving affectionate wife, with whom I could share my heart and soul, were dashed to the ground. I think she's a bit cracked and suffers from a disease called Cod."

"What's that?" Sheela had never heard of such an ailment.

"it means Compulsory Obsessive Disease. She's obssessed with certain trifling matters, which she somehow cannot get out of her mind, as a result of which she gets easily irritated. The first night I wanted to make love to her, she said no, it is Monday and I have to do my pujas. After her pujas, I approached her again but she refused on the pretext that doing sex on that particular day would defile her body because already 'sankranti' had set in after 12 o'clock in the night and that it was already 1 a.m. and all that rubbish and all that blah blah blah which I can never understand. I felt like slapping her there and then." He glanced at Sheela and she was yawning. "Are you feeling bored, my dear?"

"No,no, not at all. Its just that I didn't sleep well last night; the excitement of meeting you was so great. Well, your wife's disease is a very common one which many women suffer from. To be frank with you Ravi, I don't want you to talk ill of your wife. I feel guilty because I feel I am the one who has spoiled your family life and developed in you a hatred for her. You've always said lets enjoy the present,why talk of the past?"

A tinge of annoyance shadowed Ravi's face. "But Sheela, try to understand. Till now, I haven't told about my misery to anyone in this world. Her parents and my acquaintances know we are quite happy. But God only knows how miserable I am with her. And I have to tell this to someone, and who else other than you? Why should anyone listen to or understand my problems? You are mine, my very own, and therefore you have to listen to me. You are the only person to whom I can bare my soul; therefore Sheela, please listen to me, at least for my sake, for making me feel better. During the first few months of our marriage, whenever I approached her for sex, she just avoided me, saying since I had eaten non-veg, I could not even touch her. She's crazy, yaar. And one fine day, I don't know what came over her, she said I would have to become a total vegetarian because some Sadhu Baba had told her it would be good for my career. I said to hell with my career and first I need to satisfy my basic wants which are good food and sex; and that if she would not satisfy me, I would go to a prostitute or call-girl. After that she changed, and when my son was conceived, I was happy that I would be a father and not just a husband to a lousy log. She's indeed a horrible lady amd makes life hell not only for me,but also my son, who has to obey her innumerable dos and donts." He spat bitter venom against his wife throughout the journey, and Sheela could not but listen to him patiently. At last, she said,

"Have patience,darling, after all, she is your wife."

Ravi looked desperately at her, "If you agree to marry me, I'll easily give her a divorce."

"O no, it'll lead to many problems." Sheela knew Ravi would lose no time in taking the plunge once she gave him the green signal. But she didn't have the guts to walk out of her marriage, which was her comfortable zone. Besides, there was her little son, Raja. How could she leave him? "Come on, Ravi, be happy. We are quite comfortable as we are."

"Okay, I'll be happy and cool down, as you wish." He laughed. "You see, whenever I feel angry, I always think about you and it gives me immense pleasure, Somehow, the picture of your sweet face gives me the strength to live, like Wordsworth felt when he contemplated about nature, or imagined the still,calm beauty of Tintern Abbey." He kissed her softly on her cheeks.

"Ravi, what are you doing? Be careful, you are driving." Sheela pushed him away. ""Now tell me, why didn't you come and propose to me before marrying.? My parents would have readily agreed"

"How could I?" Ravi's mood changed and There was a terrible pain in his voice. Sheela regretted having asked him

"I'm sorry, Ravi. Forget it. Let bygones be bygones. Let's enjoy the present."

"No, Sheela, you must know about the whole incident." He stopped the car at a wayside hotel "Let's eat something here and in the meantime, I'll tell you the whole story." They sat at the dining and ordered for snacks and coffee. ". You know how my parents died in an accident twenty years ago. Then,You and your parents bade me goodbye at Chandnagar station, when me and my sister Ranji were snatched away from you by my uncle to be taken to Kerala. Ranji was forcibly married off to an old man. We had a lot of landed property there, but lest I grow up and claim my share of the land, they sent me off to Riyadh, to work as a labourer, imagine,at the age of fifteen."

"How could your own uncle, your father's brother be so cruel?" Sheela asked surprised

"Well, it's the greed of property, my dear, which make people blind. People find it strange that it's the loved and close ones who are jealous and envious. But it's only the near ones who can be jealous; because closeness implies jealousy. Jealousy won't come to me if a person whom I don't know gets a promotion. But if one of my colleagues gets a promotion, green envy starts eating me up. Well, it was terrible, those hard-working days at Riyadh, and one day I fell sick. An Indian doctor had come to treat us, and while he was examining me, I requested him to take me away from there and make me his servant. He took pity on me and somehow managed to convince the brick-kiln owner that my health would not permit me to work there any longer. The owner, of course, was kind enough to relieve me of my duties there."

"Then what happened?" Sheela was listening to him in rapt attention, in between sips of coffee.

"I worked in the doctor's house and when they came to India, they brought me along with them. I vowed I would never leave India again."

"For how many years you stayed there?" Sheela took his hand in hers and held it.

"Almost two years." Ravi stared at Sheela and looked deep into her eyes. "And every moment of those two years, I thought of you and yearned to be near you. And when every moment was a pain, then memories of the wonderful time during my childhood and early teenage with you erased my pain. Did you often think of me, my dear?"

Sheela looked hurt. "Ravi, how can you doubt it when you know how much I feel for you. I was wondering why you didn't write to me from Kerala. We didn't have a land phone and the cell hadn't been invented Everyday, I asked the postman if there was a letter for me, but he always replied no"

Ravi looked surprised. "But I wrote to you from Riyadh always at an interval of one or two months. And when no reply came, I presumed you didn't want to be in touch with me. I felt miserable and then I realized how much I loved you and life without you would be unbearable."

"But those letters never reached me, and I thought you had forgotten me. I tried my best to get your uncle's address through some acquaintances and that distant aunt of yours, but to no avail But still I hoped one day you'll come and definitely propose to me"

"Never hope or want, Sheela; for hopes lead to despair and wants lead to disappointments. And never pray to God for anything, for it only leads to suffering and pain making us go through endless rituals, and life becomes a painful journey. You can't enjoy life at all if you keep on wanting always. Therefore, I've learnt not to want, or hope, or desire, but only to accept. When hope bubbles up, I just try to pluck it out and throw it out of my mind.

Sheela could understand, for she herself had become a stoic, just accepting her destiny. But now she was more interested in knowing about the happenings in Ravi' s life. "Did the doctor and his family go back to Riyadh again?"

"Yes, after two months of holidaying at India, they went back. But I didn't go with them.

Instead, I worked as a waiter in a Mumbai five star hotel. At that time, I was only eighteen years old. Till late in the night, I used to study hard, and then I took my class XII exams privately"

"But why didn't you come to us? You know my parents would always help you. You could have stayed with us." By now they had finished eating.

"Let's go to a room. I'm feeling very tired, and I just want to relax a bit"

Sheela looked dismayed. "but Ravi, we'll be late for home. My father will be worried."

"Thirty minutes or one hour late won't make any difference." Ravi appeared stern. "I can't drive right now. I need a little rest."

He strode to the counter and booked a room. Inside the room, they stretched out their arms and legs and relaxed on the sofa. "yes, where was I? I could have stayed with you and your parents, you said. I know, darling, I know. But every moment was a pain in the heart and soul and I didn't want to dump my depression on you. I became determined to study hard and do a good job. I loved you and I knew, with you beside me, I could never concentrate on studies because romance at that young age would drown my ambition a nd perseverance. I decided after getting a good job, I would go to you"

"You got a first division in your class xii board?"

"Of course! For three years after that, I struggled and laboured very hard. It was a rigorous 'tapasya', a 'sadhana' for me. I bought books with the money I got from my salary, and along with preparation for my graduation, I also studied for the civil services, bank P.O, and other competitive exams. My only aim was to get a good job and then marry you." Sheela felt interested and listened to him attentively as the hardships of his life became unraveled before her.

"Well, even if you wouldn't have got a job, I would have still married you. I could have done a job and we would be happy together. After all, when there is love, money is not a big deal."

"I know money is not everything," Ravi acquiesced. "But some amount of money is indeed necessary in order to be happy in life. O, what a happy day it was when I received my appointment letter as a probationary officer in Canara Bank. I was overjoyed because I could marry you.". Then his face saddened. "But fate intervened, Sheela fate. What we imagine never happens. What we dream never comes true. There's only hopelessness and despair." And he beat his fist against the table.

"Ravi, don't be so childish." Sheela reprimanded. "Why should there be despair?. I am near you always."

He turned to her, held her by her shoulders and shrugged her hard. "Tell me, will you marry me now?. If you love me so much, divorce your husband and marry me, so that we don't have to meet and make love hidingly and secretly" He looked desperately at Sheela, seeking her approval. Sheela remained quiet for some time. Then she said, "Ravi, I would have divorced my husband if I didn't love my Raja, my son so much. I can't make him miserable by breaking up my family life. Besides, marriage and divorce are only rituals ordained by our so called society. I don't believe it can be a barrier to our love. My heart and soul are with you and that is what matters."

"And what about your body?" Ravi got angry. "I want you, Sheela and 'you' means not only your heart and soul, but also your body. I knew you would make pretexts. And therefore I said there's only hopelessness and despair." Sheela thought he just raved like a mad philosopher and it would do them good if they began their journey homewards.

"Let's go", she said, standing up "Its getting late and my Papa will be worried."

"No!" He uttered, infuriated. He pulled her down and she almost fell. But she again sat down near him. "I have to tell you what happened that fateful night. Are you listening?"

"Yes."

The picture came back vividly to Ravi's memory. "It was the second week of our training at Gurgaon. I was trying to find the ealiest opportunity to come to your parents and seek your hand. I had applied for two days leave after a month of training and my boss had agreed. The following day, I was supposed to come to your place by flight and seek your hand for I had already booked a seat in the jet airways. But fate had something horrible in store for me."

"Then what happened" Sheela felt interested.

"That evening itself, my boss was preparing himself to attend the wedding ceremony of the local MLA's daughter which was being held at a farmhouse some 60kms away from Gurgaon,when all of a sudden, he fell sick with diarhooea, accompanied with high fever. I rushed him to the nearest nursing home, and when he felt a bit better, he requested me to attend the marriage on his behalf. He put Rs.1000 in a gift packet, wrote his name and requested me to go and hand it over to the MLA. I went in the bank's jeep, and after gulping down a tasty and sumptuous dinner, I took my leave of them and had just started my return journey in the jeep, when the news arrived that the bridegroom and his party had met with a severe accident and the bridegroom had died. Immediately, the relatives of the MLA rushed to me and halted my start. Are you married ? they asked. I said no, and then the MLA himself came and requested me to marry his plump and not-so-beautiful daughter. When I refused, his men grabbed me and forcibly, at gun point, they led me to the altar. I said I would rather be killed by them than marry her. Instead,they forcibly made me gulp some drink and I fainted. In that unconscious state, two sturdy men held me and made me sit on the altar and according to vedic rites, I got married. On getting back my senses, when I saw the video clips, everything seemed so absurd, so nightmarish. The next morning, in the five star hotel room, when I heard "I am your wife, you have to live with me forever", I felt like committing suicide. However, dropping her in my in-laws house that day itself, I rushed back to Gurgaon to continue with my training. After completion, when I was appointed at Mumbai, I rented a flat and brought my wife to stay with me. Really, life has been hellish with her".

Sheela took his hand in hers. "Ravi, let's forget the past. The past is gone. Why remember it again and again and spoil the present". She snuggled up close to him, and hugging him, kissed him on his cheeks.

Ravi cheered up. "Then lets make love today, just now. Come on, Sheela, be a sport; help me to feel better and relaxed."

"No, Ravi," Sheela looked at her watch. "My God, it's already past 6. By the time I reach home, it'll be 7.30 or 8 p.m. Papa will be getting worried" She got up from the sofa to move towards the door, but a small, beautiful candle stand on the table caught her attention. She picked it up and examined it. "It's lovely, isn't it Ravi, but there's no candle in it". Just then, she felt Ravi's body pressing against her back and his hands groping her. "Ravi, please, not now", but a moment later, his lips were on hers and he was pushing her onto the bed. After that, he had no control over what had happened. At first, Sheela was hesitant, but as he took out her clothes and plunged into her, joyful screams emanated naturally. "O yes, its wonderful. Do it like that, Ravi. My God, its been almost more than a month since I've had it, and that too,with you." Then finally both of them gasped with joy and exhaustion and he kissed her passionately. "O darling Sheela, I love you."

Sheela lay on the bed, blissful for a minute or two, savoring every nuance of the flavour of love. Gradually, realization dawned on her that it was getting late; and strangely, her conscience pricked her again and she thought she was committing a sin in deviating from her marriage vows. "What am I doing? If my husband finds out, I'll be finished"

Ravi, as though reading her mind, rebuked her. "Don't look so cheerless. Your husband'll never know. It'll be our little secret."

Sheela stared into Ravi's eyes and jumped straight into his arms. There was something about him, so attractive, so magnetic that she could not resist herself. "How can I make you happy, dear?" she asked passionately.

"By giving yourself to me, entirely." Then they made love. It was a wonderful union, a coming together that produced an exquisite joy and mirth in Sheela which she had never dreamed would be possible. The room, the world, the universe, everything rocked for the lovers as though an earthquake was taking place, until there was a delirious, ecstatic explosion.

The unbelievably marvelous journey ended, leaving them shattered, spent and numb. Sheela lay there, holding Ravi tightly, wanting the feeling to continue, and wanting him to be beside her always. Now, it was Ravi's turn to initiate their going. "Let's make a move. It's getting late." He said. After checking out and paying the bill, Ravi, with Sheela beside him started the return journey.

It was almost 11p.m. when Sheela reached home. Before dropping her, Ravi said, "Sheela, tomorrow, we must make love again, and no excuses. I am dying for it."

Sheela put her hands on his lips." Don't utter that word. Rather you should say I am living for it. May you live for more than a hundred years. And bye! See you tomorrow." She went in and kissed her sleeping son lightly on his cheeks. Then she relaxed on the sofa, enjoying in her thoughts and whole being the flavour of Ravi's presence.

"Sheela," her father broke in upon her thoughts. "Your husband had rung up and I told him you were out. He seemed a bit annoyed. however, I forgot your cell no. Anyway, you must be tired. Have your dinner and go to sleep."

"Papa, I had some sort of high tea with my friend just a couple of hours ago. I'm not hungry. Did Raja miss me?"

"No, no, why should he miss you when his grandparents are here?," and he laughed heartily." He just asked where you had gone, and cribbed that he could have gone with you, but somehow I pacified him with a chocolate, a visit to the park and two lovely ice-creams."

"But Papa, he'll catch cold and fall sick if he eats so many ice-creams. You know he has tonsillitis."

Her Papa laughed. "No, my dear. Rest assured he'll not fall sick. I remember when you were a child like him, you used to eat so many ice-creams, but you never fell sick" And he merrily chatted about those good old days when sometimes he used to bring Sheela home from school in his cycle, and they would stop by to lick Gaylord ice-creams from the ice-cream vendor. Their topic soon veered to something humorous about their neighbours,and when her mother dropped in, both father and daughter were laughing heartily. "Sheela, stop gossiping so much. Now eat something and go to sleep. You look very tired and certainly you need rest." But Sheela was in high spirits and felt very cheerful. It was wonderful being with Ravi and she wanted to enjoy the hangover of his togetherness. She just ate a bit and slept soundly throughout the night.

12

The next day, Ravi was waiting as usual at the appointed place. Ravi's face lit up at spotting her amidst the crowd. "My God! You're looking gorgeous. What with a bright red sari and a red bindiya. Really, you look like a bride. I'd always imagined you to be coming like this to me. And see, it has come true. At times, wishes do come true, isn't it,my dear." And he clasped her hand tightly, as if totally possessing her and declaring to the world that no one could snatch her away from him. "Come on, le'sget away from here. I've already booked a hotel; we shoudn't waste time"

"But Ravi, I'm hungry. I haven't had lunch." Sheela said

"Then we can order lunch in the room itself. Come along."

They fled amidst the crowd to the room in the hotel Sheela ate slowly, savouring every item. "Sheela, hurry up. I can't wait longer to do----you know what "and he winked at her. Then he kissed her forehead and hugged her close to himself. "Ravi, let me at least finish my lunch and wash my hands and mouth, and then we'll do—you know what" and she burst out laughing, not so much at her own words, but because of the excitement at beginning a journey once again into the forbidden and uncharted territory of love—a journey in which they would only explore and explore and make newer discoveries of the feeling of love. After she had washed up. Ravi pulled her up to the bed and laying her down with her face upwards, he started showering her with kisses, from her head to her toes, first gently, then passionately and finally ecstatically. It was a joyous moment for Ravi.

At first he was climbing, and then flying with wings outstretched up to the peak of the mountain, like a fledgling who has just come out of its shell and discovered there was so mich power in him, flying with an innocent, pure freedom, far away from bondage. Such wonder he had never experienced before. It was a pure unalloyed, unadulterated bliss on realizing he had so much energy in him to love, to give love and derive pleasure by giving. Sheela lay on the bed, spellbound by the amazing beauty of this wonderful adventure, her parched body thrilled by the touch of the tender shower of kisses,a soft bloom emanating out of her whole being. She too began flying with him, exploring this realm of love and freedom, and enjoying the discovery of every nook and corner of this most beautiful territory. And when they had plunged and entered into the domain surrounding the peak, and were just about to each the climax, her cell rang. Sheela's joyous spell broke and she said softly. "Ravi, my mobile is ringing."

"To hell with it! Let it ring. Why didn't you switch it off?"

"But Ravi, maybe its urgent." And she pushd him away, got up and reached for her purse. She took out the phone and when she saw the number a look of dismay swept across her face.

"Who's it?" Ravi asked disgustedly, angry with Sheela for letting him down when he was just beginning to reach the climax.

' My husband", and the phone kept on ringing loudly forcing her to click it on." Hello."

"Sheela!" Her husband's voice rang out loud and clear. "Where are you? I've been calling for so long and you aren't even clicking it. Why you so absent-minded? What are you doing?"

Ravi was about to say something when Sheela put her hands on his lips and body language suggested that he should remain quiet, lest her husband recognize a male voice. "Er-----I'm in Binny's place. Where are you? In the office?"

"No, you fool. I'm right in your father's house at BBSR My mother was suddenly diagnosed with kidney failure, and she is at our hme in Kolkata. My sisters are with her. I've come here to take you back home to Kolkata. Tell me where you are, and I'll go by your father's scooter and bring you."

"No, no why take the pains. I'll go by auto." And Sheela was shocked and angry. Even in her wildest imagination, she had never thought of such a negative possibility. It seemed fate was conniving with her husband to deprive her of the little happiness and enjoyment in her lot. Ravi stared at her, totally confused,and then pulled her close and kissed her passionately.

She pushed him away. "Ravi, I have to go immediately. I'll tell you the details as we go. It seems destiny doesn't want us to be together."

They walked silently along the corridors of the hotel and then Ravi blurted out, "Its really unfair! Why amongst all the people in the world did God choose us to suffer like this? We love each other,but we can't be together. Its absurd, horrible, I say." Sheela clasped his hands tightly, and a kind of closeness which she had never felt before sprang up in her veins. She smiled at Ravi, patience written all ove her face. "Take it easy, Ravi. You know the course of true love never runs smooth. Had it been smooth sailing, Laila-Majnu, Romeo-Juliet, Heer-Ranjha, would not have died for the sake of love. Or perhaps had it been smooth-sailing, there would be no charm in it, and love would have deteriorated into commonness and a routine affair. Maybe if we had married, we wouldn't have enjoyed loving each other so much . . ."

"Nonsense! I don't believe it at all! I'll show to the world that the course of true love does run smooth and show them how we'll be blissfully happy together too. I'm thinking of getting a divorce and you must get one too".

Sheela stopped and stared at him, horrified. "how can you say such a thing! Divorce? Impossible! Think of all the legal battles we have to fight and the hassles we have to face. It'll leave us very little time for mental peace and thinking or feeling love for each other at all. And what about your son or my son? Won't we be depriving them of our love and care to which they have a right. The hangover of a guilty conscience of unnecessarily putting our sons into trouble, will leave us very little space for mental peace. And if there's no mental peace, from where will love spring up? No Ravi, never think of divorce."

Suddenly, Ravi turned around and held her by her shoulders. He looked deep into her eyes and said fiercely, "Then you won't divorce your husband. You are afraid of him, I'm sure. Your fear of him outweighs your love for me. You are not as brave as I thought, Sheela. You are not at all a brave woman."

"Its not a question of bravery or love. Our lives will become hell after divorcing our respective spouses. Why don't you understand?" Sheela felt exasperated.

"Then you mean to say that throughout our lives we'll be playing a game of hide and seek, hide from the world while seeking each other,loving but not expressing it, love without fulfillment or consummation. What kind of relationship is this? I say its sheer hypocrisy and I really don't like it." His temper was rising, and Sheela stared at him for long, long enough for Ravi to catch the infection of patience and affection for him which brimmed over in her eyes. At last, she smiled and said "Now look, there's a great pleasure in playing this hide and seek game. It makes us feel so young and childlike, like two, innocent, teenage lovers. Its indeed wonderful,cheating and defying the world. Besides, there's great joy in just loving, without hope or expectation of anything. Marriage brings in a lot of expectations. You see, whenever I feel miserable, frustrated or depressed, I just think of you, imagine you and all my sorrows vanish into thin air. Love brings a lot of happiness, Ravi, it never brings pain. And there is great power in love too. It subdues all your sorrow and makes you adjust to any circumstance in the world. Your love has truly given that power within me."

Ravi listened to her, staring at her wide-eyed with wonder. His face then glowed with a childish excitement. "You really feel like that? I have felt the same too whenever I have thought about you. That means we truly love each other. We've found true love. Eureka! It's the rarest of rare treasure. O Sheela, I'm so happy today." And his face kept on glowing with joy and there was a lightness and a sprightliness in his gait,which she had never observed before,as though he was dancing

"Okay, well, then never think of divorce, right?" Sheela tutored him as though he was a truant student escaping his studies. Just then,her cell rang. By now, they had reached the exit and Sheela was hailing an auto. "Sheela, when are you reaching? It's getting late. We have to go." Her husband's voice sounded irritated.

Sheela was surprised. "I'm reaching within ten minutes. Anyway,where do we have to go just now?"

"I just can't talk so much over the phone. Just reach home and you'll know."

Sitting inside the auto, Sheela felt anxious, but she forced herself to smile at Ravi as she waved him goodbye. On reaching home, she was drenched by a tirade of questions showered by her husband. "Sheela, where had you been? Why didn't you take Raja? Are you mad? Where had you gone yesterday also leaving behind our little Raja? Is your friend so very important?" and so on and on.

Sheela just listened, struggling hard to keep her anger within limits. She felt like charging at him like an angry lion, but she restrained herself, for she knew it would not be wise. "I had been to a friend's house." She deliberately tried to be very casual.

"What sort of a friend is she? Is she so very important? You had said that you wanted to spend time with your parents. But you've hardly spent any time with them. Rather, you've only been visiting friends. Whenever I ring up, you're not at home and your mother says that you are at a friend's."

Sheela tried todivert him. "Anyway, did you have tea and snacks? I'll help Ma to prepare the meal.".

"Meal? No, not at all. It's already 4 o' clock. And the train is at a quarter to five. There's absolutely no time to waste. Pack up your things and hurry up."

"But why should I go now? You said I would go on Sunday evening. And the ticket has been made too. Its outrageous.!" For once, Sheela felt brave enough to challenge her husband's decision.

"But why should I go?" Her husband mimicked her sarcastically. "Don't you know? Ma is very sick; and she's come to Kolkata for treatment. My sisters have also come to look after her. Who is to cook for them while they are busy attending to my mother, or taking her to the hospital or the doctor?. You know how expensive eating out is,and therefore they will naturally eat their meals at home. Certainly, you've got to be at home." And he stared at her angrily, making his eyes as big as possible. Sheela wanted to argue with him,explaining to him that he should appoint a cook for some days, and that she was not just a maid-servant in their house. But she knew it would fall on deaf ears and therefore she remained quiet. In fact, she realized she lacked the courage to say so. Just then, her father and son entered the room and her husband softened his tone. "Now come on, Sheela, get ready and let's go."

"Papa, I have to go now," Sheela said and tears brimmed up in her eyes.

"But why today? You said you would go on Sunday, in the night!" Sheela's father liked his grandson's company and wished he would stay another day.

"ma is sick and my sisters-in-law are there at our house to look after her. And who's there to look after all of them! And so I have to go." A tear rolled down her cheeks. Raja ran and clinging to his mother wailed "Ma, let us not go today, please, I want to stay. We can go on Sunday."

"Tell your father. If he is kind and gracious enough to allow us, we'll stay." Sheela was sarcastic.

"No,my dear, we cannot stay. Your grandma's very sick and she wants us to be with her. Now, be a good boy. Eat up your biscuits and drink the milk. I'm hiring an auto. Let's go soon, or else we'll miss the train."

While boarding the train, Sheela's eyes fell on her father, and she could no longer restrain herself. Tears streamed down her cheeks and she wept bitterly; Her father patted her,trying to console her. "No no, my dear, don't cry so much. You have your cell. You can ring me up whenever you like. And Kolkata is so near too. You can come whenever you like."

"No Papa, I can't. It's like a jail." And again, there was an outburst as she bared out her painful heart to her father.

"Sheela, whatever has come over you? Why are you crying hysterically like this? He husband rebuked. "It's a station and people are staring at you. As if you are a newly-wed. Stop it, I say." Sheela wiped away her tears, and emboldened by her father's presence,she stared at her husband hatefully, her eyes red. How would he know or even understand her pain and suffering! He had the heart of a beast with very little feeling and compassion—a real killjoy. Not only was there the misery of separation from her parents, but also the curtailment of her enjoyment of Ravi's presence for another day. The train began to move and her father rushed out of the compartment. As the train chugged along,she waved goodbye to her father till as long as she could see.

Raja cried out excitedly, "Lok mama, what a cute little hut there is over those hills, Look mama!" Sheela glanced absent-mindedly. Her mind was faraway, to Ravi. How cruel destiny was! A slight twist of fate got her married to this man, so unfeeling, indifferent and dispassionate. She looked at him. He was lost in his own thoughts, and didn't even care to ask if she would like to eat something. Just then, her cell rang and she was dismayed to see Ravi's number. She quickly switched it off.

"You should have answered the call." Her husband chided her mildly. "Anyway, who was it?"

"My father"

"Why did you switch it off then. Its very indecent, really. He might have wanted to know something. I'm calling him back."

Her husband's mobile was in the loud mode. Sheela strained her ears to listen to what her father was saying. "Hello! Where have you reached?"

"We are just entering into Sundara Station. Want to talk with Sheela?"

"No,no, its okay! I was just thinking of ringing you up when you called."

"But you made a call to Sheela just now, I think."

"No, no, not at all. However, inform me when you reach Kolkata. Happy journey!" And he switched off.

Her husband looked at Sheela "Your father says he didn't ring you up?"

Sheela pretended to have a headache. She contorted her brows and made a painful face, massaging her forehead with her fingers and reclining her head on the window-sill. "I don't know. I thought it was Papa's number.

Whosoever it was, I didn't feel like talking. My head is throbbing terribly." And she just shut her eyes trying to sleep.

"Take a saridon tablet. But eat something first. O yes, I forgot to tell you; your mother packed some puris and dum aloo in a polythene bag while I was leaving home. I've put them in that bag. I'll take out and serve you just now."

"No, I don't feel like eating anything," though her tummy was yawning with hunger. "I'm feeling nausea and I want to sleep.". She shut her eyes and pretended to fall asleep. Her husband thought it best to leave her alone and soon became engrossed in thoughts about his ailing mother.

13

At home in Kolkata, Sheela was confronted with a dismal scene. Her sisters-in-law were waiting for her arrival, and her mother-in-law was lying on the bed, groaning with pain. Putting down her bag, she rushed to the kitchen and prepared tea for her in-laws and husband. She was surprised at her guilt feeling, a feeling of shame that she was neglecting her duties. It was as though her in-laws were waiting for an explanation from her as to why she left without notice. Only in offices, the explanation was demanded in written, while here it was unwritten. She was just a servant, or rather a slave; for servants were at least paid, but she was unpaid. She had signed the contract of being a bonded labourer throughout her life on the day of her marriage itself. And therefore it was of no use complaining.

"What disease is Maa suffering from? What do the doctors say?" Sheela asked Kajol while they were having dinner. Her mind and body ached for rest, but she continued to put up an appearance of being a dutiful daughter-in-law.

"Some kidney problem, they say. There's a tumour inside her kidney which needs to be operated. immediately. Plus, her blood pressure and sugar levels are quite high. You never come to the village, so how will you know?" Her sister-in-law said accusingly.

But Sheela was not to be daunted. "How will I go? Your brother doesn't allow me to go anywhere. I went to my father's house after a gap of six months, and you just saw how he brought me back after a stay of only two days. Is it fair and just?" Both her sisters-in-law laughed, but Sheela couldn't know whether there was sarcasm or humour in the words when one of them said, "O, our brother loves you too much. Therefore he cannot live without you and wants to keep you near him always." Anger was seething within Sheela, but she did not express it on her face or her behaviour. Silently and dutifully, she returned to her nocturnal chores, letting out a yawn now and then. As she lay down to sleep, her thoughts went to Ravi, and she felt annoyed with her husband for depriving her of some moments of joy with Ravi. Soon, sleep overcame her tired body and she was lost in the world of dreams.

Ravi didn't call up to Sheela for almost a month and she felt anxious. Surely Ravi remembered the time, between 11 a.m-3 p.m during which he could make a call on any working day, except Saturday. Was he annoyed with her? She wondered. But then, he was so sensible, understanding and level-headed. Certainly, he would understand. Most of the time, she was distracted, and her mind involuntarily wandered to Ravi, though she continued to serve her husband and in-laws docilely. Meanwhile, the cancerous tumour in her mother-in-law's kidney grew by leaps and bounds and the doctor announced a particular day when she would be operated upon. It was the 30ᵗʰ of July, only a ten days away, and her husband remained busy arranging money for the operation. So much so that he had no time or the inclination to pick up the petty quarrels with Sheela, which he used to do quite often. He was a typical mama's boy and could not bear to see his mother suffer. His two sisters all the while nursed their mother while Sheela had a hell of a time, burdened with too much work of home-management, cooking and other household chores.

One late evening, just a few days before the operation date, Sheela felt like nursing her mother-in-law. She knew the old lady's days were numbered, and this was just a slight opportunity to nurse her and be close to her. She sat down to massage the old lady's legs and realized how thin, helpless and fragile she looked, as she lay there, crumpled up in a heap. Truly, destiny can make a prince of a pauper and a pauper of a prince at any moment. Or maybe it is character, or choice made by free will which brings about this curious and mysterious quirk of fate? Whatever it is, this lady was once the matriarch of the house, the undisputed queen of her home, most of the time shouting and shrieking at the top of her voice, imposing her dominant will not only on her husband when he was alive, but also on her son and everybody else in the house. Perhaps the fear of being a henpecked husband like his father had made Sheela's husband more aggressive in his behaviour towards Sheela. As she watched the rapid breathing body, the old lady opened her dull, pale eyes and beckoned to Sheela to come closer to her. Her voice was faint and hardly audible as she spoke. "Daughter-in-law, most of the time, I haven't treated you well. Much as I would have liked to repent and make it up with you, there is no opportunity for it now, because I have a few days to live. But please bear in mind that you have been a good daughter-in-law and my blessings are always with you."

"No, no, Ma, please don't think that your days are numbered. You'll live very long; besides, it is such a minor operation too. You'll get well soon." But the old lady did not hear. She had already closed her eyes, as if opening her eyes and uttering those words had drained out all her energy.

The next day began with bright sunshine and Sheela was still wondering why Ravi hadn't given her a call for so long. It was a Saturday and her husband was sitting near his mother, and on the pretext of buying some vegetables, Sheela went to the market. Taking shelter from the blazing sun in the foyer of a market complex, she dialled Ravi's number on her cell. "Hello, Ravi, its Sheela here. Why haven't you rung me up all these days? Are you angry with me?"

"O my God! Can I ever be angry with you, my dear dear Sheela! Actually I had rung you up some days ago sometime in the late morning, just after 11 a.m. Your husband received it and I pretended as though it was a wrong number. After that, I dared not ring you up, lest your husband receives it again. Anyway, how are you? I've got wonderful news for you."

"Really! About whom? And what?"

"About ourselves, of course! What else can be wonderful for us? I was just thinking of giving you a call on Monday; thankfully you did it. Guess what is the news?"

"I'm sure you've got a promotion. And congratulations for it." Sheela said excitedly.

"No, my dear; Keep on guessing."

For a moment or two, Sheela remained quiet. And then she said, "I give up. Tell me what it is?"

"It's this, that I've got a tour programme to Kolkata on the 30th of this month. I'll reach there by flight at half-past nine, and after a meeting with the CGM, I'll become free by 2 o' clock in the afternoon. You can meet me then. We can have lunch and be together for some time. Isn't that great, my dear!"

Sheela's heart sank. 30th was the day of her mother-in-law's operation and she had to keep vigil either at her home or in the nursing home. "But

Ravi, can't we meet on the 31ˢᵗ or the 1ˢᵗ of August or perhaps even later when you come next time?"

"Come on Sheela, don't be silly. Don't you know that bank officers don't enjoy so many leaves or holidays.? My return flight is booked on the 30ᵗʰ itself at 6 p. m., and I have to be present in a very important bank meeting the next day. Besides, I have a very urgent and important meeting here on 30ᵗʰ night related to our apartment registration. The bank won't excuse my staying back, even if it is for one day. Therefore, I have to return on the 30ᵗʰ itself."

"But Ravi, its not possible for me to meet you on that day." Sheela's voice cracked over the phone.

"Why? What's wrong.?"

"My mother-in-law will undergo a major operation on that particular day. It will start at 1 O' clock in the afternoon and will continue till perhaps 6 p. m. in the evening and during that particular time, I cannot move out at all. Naturally, I'll be busy throughout the day and my services will be indispensable. I can't neglect my duties at home. Please Ravi, forgive me this time; I'll never let you down next time".

"Really Sheela, I'm fed up of your ways. Why at all did you revive this relationship when it had completely died down and had become a mere memory? I've come to meet you twice, first at Kolkata,and then at BBSR. And each time, in some way or the other, you've left me in the lurch. First time, you kept me waiting at the bus-stop. Next, in BBSR too, you left me midway. And this time also, you are making excuses. It's too much, really. What's the point in loving me and then giving me pain and unhappiness. Love means a lot of sacrifices, taking risks, and then only one can feel one's love and enjoy it too. Besides, that's the only day when I can meet you before going to the USA on the 7ᵗʰ of August of this year. And I'll be staying at USA for a year or so. So it'll be very long before I can see you again."

"Please Ravi, don't misunderstand me. It's very easy for you to come and meet me since you are a man. But I'm an Indian woman and not a western lady." Sheela blurted out angrily. She felt irritated with Ravi for insisting only on his point of view. "You don't realize my problem. If you truly love me, you would sympathize with me and not be anxious for sex."

Ravi became furious. "What do you mean? Anxious for sex, huh, like a mere animal. Had I been eager for sex, I could have had it with any pretty woman. But why am I mad for your company? Because I love you, and only you in this world and I want to express and enjoy loving you, even if I have to make sacrifices. How can you be so old-fashioned and stupid to say I love you only to have sex.?"

Sheela never expected that Ravi would argue with her like this and rebuke her. She realized he was some sort of a rebel and was always determined to carry out his decision.

"But Ravi, you don't understand my problem. On that particular day and time, my mother-in-law will be battling between life and death, and I'll be enjoying myself with my lover.! Doesn't it sound weird and absurd! Somehow it doesn't sound right to me. I always believed you were so sensible and intelligent, and never imagined you could be so foolish." She gave him a piece of her mind.

"Well, let's not quarrel about it anymore. Tell me, whether you are coming or not. If you come, it will be proof enough that you truly love me. And we will continue our relationship till I come up with a solution as to how we can remain together as long as we live. If you don't come, I'll take it for granted that you don't love me. Rest assured that I love you and will do so throughout my life and never think of any other woman. But I won't let you ignite me, burn me and then leave me half-burnt. Its very painful. Rather, I'll keep you in my memory and heart forever and worship you there, if that is what you want—a sort of platonic love. Hello, are you listening?"

"Yes", Sheela said feebly. But actually she was not very attentive to what Ravi was saying. The burden of working hard at home-making for the comfort of her in-laws, husband and son was taking a toll on her nerves and she was too fatigued to argue any more.

"And remember. If you don't turn up on that day, you'll never hear from me again because I can no longer bear the pain of unfulfilment. Always making up excuses about your husband or in-laws, etc. Why the hell did you revive this relationship if you were not prepared to brave hurdles or make sacrifices? It's like going almost to the top of the mountain and being pushed down from there, before reaching the peak. Well, I'm expecting you on that day at 2 p. m, at our usual venue, the bus-stop, and if you don't turn up, never hope to see me again or hear from me." And he switched off. Sheela sat down on a bench in the foyer and wiped of the beads of perspiration on her forehead. It was a sultry hot noon, with no sign of wind, but a storm was brewing up within her. It was a feeling of helplessness. And it whirled her within its vortex and completely threw her off her guard. She was between the devil and the deep sea, a Scylla and the Charybdis—a Hamletian dilemma, to do or not to do. It was getting late and she had better go. She picked up her purchases and slowly walked towards her home—or rather her husband's home. If she didn't oblige Ravi she would lose his love and her love and life forever—for Ravi was her life too. On the other hand, if she would not stay either at home or the nursing home during her mother-in-laws operation, her sisters-in-law and her husband would raise a storm terrible enough to make her feel miserable. No, she could not afford to lose Ravi; not at any cost. He was the only ray of sunshine in her loveless life. Certainly, there was some way out. She thought hard and somehow hit upon a plan. Reaching home, she was tiraded by a volley of questions. "My God! Boudi! Where had yougone for so long? The soup hasn't been cooked yet; you know Ma will have her lunch at half-past twelve, and it is already quarter past twelve. What were you doing in the shop?"

Sheela contorted her face as though she was suffering from some pain and putting down the bag of vegetables on the floor, she sat down on a chair in a reclining position with her legs stretched out and her left hand placed on the right side of her waist

"What is the matter, boudi? Is there some kind of pain there?" asked her sister-in-law.

"Yes. I was in the shop when it began to ache. Within minutes, the pain increased terribly and the shopkeeper offered me a chair on which I sat down for a while. Then he gave me a pain-killer and a gastric tablet which I gulped down. After the pain subsided, I walked down home."

Panic got written all over the sisters-in-law's faces. "Is it still paining? What with Ma so sick, and you all of a sudden being taken ill, who will look after us? May it not be anything so serious! You consult a doctor immediately. When our brother comes, I will tell him to take you to a doctor first." The elder one said.

"No, no, you needn't worry at all. I'm sure its nothing very serious; just some gastric problem perhaps. And you need not trouble your brother either. He's the only one who's running helter-skelter for Ma's operation and treatment. As it is, he is already overburdened, both financially, physically and mentally. So don't worry him further. If m stomach aches again, I can go alone and consult any doctor, why trouble your brother again?"

"Okay, boudi, you take rest today, while both of us will complete the cooking and do all the other household chores. I'm only praying that there may be nothing wrong with you."

"No,no, I'm well enough to do the housework. As it is, you hardly have time;you have to nurse Ma, bathe her, feed her, clothe her from time to time. Who will do that if you do the household work? Rather I'm doing it, just as I am doing it every day. It won't be a problem for me." Saying this, Sheela went indoors to continue with her management of the house. Inwardly, she marveled at her talent in play-acting. How easily they had fallen into the trap of her feigning and pretension. She deliberately brushed aside all feelings of guilt which accused her of being a liar and a pretender, because she knew that the more she thought of her sin, the more it would overpower her and prevent her from meeting Ravi. She sent a silent prayer to God to forgive her.

14

Another three days were left for the operation and also for Ravi's arrival. Sheela had to do something or else she would forgo her claim and right over Ravi's love forever. She came to know that on this day, her husband would be busy in the office processing the formalities for getting a loan of two lakh rupees. After preparing the morning tea and serving it to one and all the members of her family, she began her stint at play action, again praying to God to be forgiven. She lay down on the bed, groaning softly, as if with pain, and contorting her face now and then. Presently, her sister-in-law came in and seeing her in this miserable condition, cried out in dismay, "Boudi, has the pain come up again? Dada, dada," she called out loudly, "come here quickly, boudi is not well."

Her dada had just come out from the bathroom after a bath and was wiping his head with a towel. He rebuked his sister, "Why are you shouting like that? What has happened to your boudi?"

"How can you be so callous, dada? Boudi's been suffering from severe pain in the stomach since the last few days and you haven't even noticed? Take her to the doctor today itself."

"Today! Impossible! Today I have to withdraw the loan and give advance to the nursing home. I'll be very busy in the office. One of you can take her to the doctor."

Sheela got up from the bed and stopped their argument. She smiled affectionately. "Okay, neither of you need take me to the doctor. I can go the doctor alone. A gynaecologist examines patients in that medicine shop at the far end of the road. She sits in the clinic on all working days from 10 a.m.-1 p.m. Retired, most probably, I can go to her.

"Okay, but today we shall do the cooking and you take rest." Her elder sister-in-law said.

"No, no, I'll do the cooking as usual. I'm feeling much better now and after finishing by half-past ten, I'll go to the doctor."

"Even though you are feeling better now, you must show the doctor. That's our order, right." And her sisters-in-law burst out laughing.

Exactly at half-past eleven in the morning, Sheela went out on the pretext of showing a doctor; actually she had some vegetables to buy, and after she had purchased some, she stood under the portico of a shop in the foyer and dialed Ravi's cell no. "hello, Ravi, it's me, your Sheela. Are you really coming to kolkata on the 30th.

"What's your problem, Sheela? It seems as though you don't want me to come. And what do you mean by 'really'.? Have I been telling you a lie these days. ? You've changed, I tell you, you've changed. Anyway, I assure you I won't take much of your time at being a dutiful and obedient daughter-in-law—just a bit of togetherness, that's all. I hope to see you that day, cheerful and smiling, and don't bring your baggage of excuses and sorrows with you. I can't bear to see you sad."

"Okay, Ravi, I'll meet you on that day. Bye." She wasn't in a mood to talk.

"You sound sad Don't worry darling, everything will be alright"

"Bye, Ravi" And she switched off.

Suddenly, she felt tired of this playacting. It was getting on her nerves; belonging to honest, lower middle-class parents, she had been built up on a strong foundation of values, she hated treachery, deceit, falsehood, negligence in duties, etc, but now it seemed she was wallowing and wading in them. She regretted having initiated their long-lost love. O, why did I write to him at all, she thought. She was between the devil and the deep. If she stood by her mother-in-law's bedside during the operation, she would lose Ravi's love. If she would go to Ravi, she may incur the wrath of her husband and her in-laws. What to do? She hoped God would bring her out of this messy situation.

15

A tense atmosphere prevailed in Sheela'a home in the morning of the operation. While she was serving breakfast to her husband, her thoughts floated to Ravi Would she be successful in going to him that day? She braved up,though with trepidation, to ask her husband while he was having his breakfast. "Shall I go to the nursing home?"

"No, you needn't.", her husband replied. "Stay at home and take care of Raja"

"But Raja has gone to school. I'll go to the gynaecologist for an ultrasound at half-past one".

"You can go tomorrow. It's not so urgent. How can you be so callous? Ma is undergoing such a major operation today. Instead of thinking about her, you are only thinking about yourself."

Not to be outdone, Sheela continued. "But the pain still persists even though I have taken the whole course of medicines. I have to go for a thorough check-up."

Sheela's sister-in-law, who was sitting beside her brother and sipping a cup of tea, came to her rescue. "Let her go, Dada, Who else is there to look after us? She has to maintain a good health. Besides, her presence is not necessary in the clinic at all. The doctors and nurses will do everything."

Thank God!, Sheela heaved a sigh, the road to Ravi is now clear and smooth. When all had left, she tidied up the kitchen and made a cup of tea for herself. At a quarter past one, she rang up to her husband and came to know that the operation had begun. She dressed up and hurried by an auto to the appointed place. Ravi was already there looking anxiously at the road. His face lit up on seeing her. "O Sheela, you really look nice." He blurted out as she got off the auto. "Let us quickly gobble up our lunch and then rush to the room in the hotel." He could sense the shadow on her face. "Why are you so glum, my dear. Don't worry, things will go off well. We'll have a heaven of a time." He took her hands in his and smiled reassuringly. "But Ravi, Sheela said sadly. "Don't you think we are committing a sin? On the one hand my mother-in-law is undergoing a major operation. They have some expectations from me too. At the same time, we'll be making love in a hotel room. Somehow, I feel it's not right."

Anger rose up in Ravi' face. Sheela could smell that he was drunk. But Ravi controlled himself." Sheela, why are you so stupid? If you remain in the nursing home, keeping vigil there, will it make any difference to your mother-in-law's treatment or operation.? Now come on, tell me, will she get well sooner? So why worry? Why don't you see my point of view? You aren't doing any harm to them or neglecting your duties. You are just enjoying a bit of love,and that too when your presence is not at all necessary to them. Besides, you have every right to enjoy this love which your husband has denied. Now come on, smile, at least for my sake." Sheela smiled feebly. They had a quick and silent lunch and rushed off to the three star hotel.

Ravi was just signing his name in the reception when Sheela whispered in his ears. "Just give your initials and my name, and not the surname."

Ravi pressed her hand reassuringly. "I'll write Mrs and mr. Ravi Kumar."

Sheela looked a bit apprehensive. "Okay, do as you wish."

Just then, a young couple came towards the counter. The lady was a foreigner and looked stunning with a black jean and a red top. The dress heightened her extremely fair complexion, while her golden brown hair glistened in the lights of the ceiling. Her companion was a young handsome Bengali guy, and their hands were locked around each other's waist. They approached laughing blissfully, absorbed in a world of their own, while the whole world was well lost for them. Ravi stared at them enviously. "Look, Sheela, how happy they are! Why can't we be like them, enjoying love and life? You'd be much better off if you'd learn something from them. I'll keep a video recording of them in my cell just to remind you always of love and life." They laughed playfully and Ravi switched on his mobile and recorded their coming together to the counter. They looked the perfect epitome of a love pair.

But Sheela wasn't listening to Ravi. Her mind was elsewhere. She was wondering if the operation was still continuing. Just then, her cell phone rang. "Sheela, is the ultrasound over.? Did you get the report? I hope nothing is wrong." It was her husband Sheela didn't know what to say. Yet she managed to say feebly.

"Er . . . . I'm still at the clinic. They've told me to wait for half-an-hour by gulping lots of water, after which they'll do the ultrasound. I'll be back within an hour with the report. Anyway, is the operation still going on?"

"Yes," and he switched off.

"O, what a beautiful bracelet you are wearing." The young lady held up Sheela's hands and looked admiringly at her stone-studded bracelet. She was speaking in an accent which was not exactly English or American. Sheela thought it was an Australian accent. "Anil darling, buy for me such a bracelet, please," and she kissed him on his cheeks.

Naturally, Anil wanted to please her. He asked Sheela. "Maa'm, from where did you get this?"

"I bought it from an antique shop in New Market. You honeymooners?

"Well, something like that. You see, we are just live-ins", and the girl giggled. "Anil darling", and the girl put her arms around her boyfriend, "buy for me such a bracelet, please, "and she kissed him on his cheeks again

"Sir," the receptionist addressed Ravi, "Here's the key. Room no. 84"

"And ours?", Anil asked as he signed.

"Room 85", the receptionist retorted. Just then, Ravi received a call and moved away into the foyer. It was an urgent call from the bank and the DGM wanted some information. Anil and his girlfriend glided away from Sheela's sight and Sheela remained standing at the counter. Hardly some seconds had gone by when two middle-aged foreign men approached the receptionist. They looked perturbed." "To which room have the couple gone?"

The receptionist stared at them surprised "which couple?"

"the Australian lady and the young Indian man"

"I can't understand whom you mean?" the receptionist retorted.

They turned to Sheela. "Maa'm, have you seen a young couple entering the hotel?" Sheela felt scared of them. They looked fierce and terrible, with spiky hair sticking out of their scalp, and red, bloodshot eyes. They were middle-aged, fat and stocky. Sheela lied. "No, I haven't". Emboldened with rage, one of them went to the receptionist and held him by his collar. "Will you tell me in which room they are?".

"Let go off me!" the receptionist shouted, pushing away his hands. "I'll call the police."

They withdrew their hands from off his collar. "I'm the lady's husband," said one and the other said, "I'm her brother. And we have every right to know where she is."

Just then, Ravi appeared and taking Sheela by the hand, they glided on the plush marble floors like two love birds in flight and entered room no. 84 and latched the door from within. Ravi pulled Sheela into his strong and virile arms and clasped her close to his heart. Sheela just melted into his body, and she became one with him, her soul touching his. For some moments, they became one soul, one body, bliss unlimited, touching the stars. Time stood still, as they were locked in kisses on the lips. And when they had drunk full delight from the lips Ravi let her off suddenly, and pulled her to the bed. He kissed her over several times, and then they made a violent, passionate love—an unbounded and limitless ocean of love. he entered and penetrated. Deep into it. And carried her along with him. Together they sailed smoothly and blissfully along the sea of life. Deeper and deeper they sailed into the ocean, moaning and groaning joyously and wonderfully at the blissful discoveries they made, exploring every nook and corner, and showering and raining love on each other like cats and dogs. Every moment was a novelty and each experience was more fulfilling than the previous one. Sheela felt wonderful, her thoughts fully suspended. For a full twenty minutes, time stood still for them. They were cut off completely from the past, present or fuure; and when they had drunk their cup of bliss till the last drop, fully satiated, they returned to the shore. Sheela gasped in delight as they separated. Ravi felt an extraordinary excitement in his blood. Sheela had never seemed so lovely, her caresses had never stirred him so powerfully, and her kisses had never seemed so ardent. And she feared nothing at that moment.

Now she realized the importance of the maxim, ' man is born free, but everywhere he is in chains'

Sheela knew that she was a prisoner, her soul trapped within her body and her body imprisoned within the society, flapping her wings in vain to be free. For her, Ravi was the symbol of freedom, for he always did whatever he wanted to do, caring a damn for what people would say, and impulsively acting according to whatever circumstances demanded, always grounded in the present. Therefore, she communicated so well with him, and her soul, her mind and feelings were as clear as crystal to him. But her husband was a prisoner, trapped in his own cage,complacent, never wanting to be free and independent, and she could never understand him or fathom his feelings, while he remained indifferent to her most of the time, and sometimes very cruel and callous. However, with a sigh, she realized she had to go back to her husband, her son, her seriously ill mother-in-law, and her sisters-in-law and play the role of a good woman in the family.

. Outside, there was a big commotion and Sheela could hear a lot of noise. "there's some trouble outside, I think. Let's quickly dress up and go."

On stepping out of the room, they saw people hurrying up and down the corridor, and somehow both could feel that the atmosphere was tense. A waiter passed by and Ravi asked "why is everyone so disturbed. What's the matter.?"

"Something horrible has happened!" The waiter said with an air of mystery around him.

"What is it?" Sheela asked alarmed.

"There has been a rape case. It seems a foreign lady who was in room no. 85 was raped by an Indian and that too an I. G.'s son. The police has arrested the young man and the lady has been taken into custody.". And the waiter rushed off.

"O my God!" blurted out Sheela. "It's the couple whom we saw coming in. How strange!"

"Sheela, let's hurry and not bother about them. Your in-laws must be waiting for you."

Just then, there was an announcement that no one could leave the hotel. They had to wait for some time and answer the queries of the police.

"O no!" Sheela cried out in dismay. They went to the counter and carried out the formalities of the checking out. The police were at the gate and questioned Ravi.

"I suppose you are Mr and Mrs. Ravi kumar who were in room no. 84 when the rape happened. Did you hear any noise or shouts of a tussle from room no. 85.?

"Er . . . . . .He is Mr. Ravi Kumar and I am Sheela Das." Sheela decided it was best to tell the truth. She knew that one lie would lead to another lie and then endless lies. Satiation had made her brave and fearless, at least for some time, and that hangover still lingered.

"You mean she is not your wife?" The policeman asked Ravi raising his eyebrows. "Then how is she related to you?"

"She's my friend," Ravi said.

"You mean a girlfriend? A lover! Huh!" He laughed mockingly. Ravi felt disgusted. "Anyway, let us go. Now that your queries are over, I'm sure we can take your leave."

"But first give your addresses and phone nos. too. And mind you, no false name or nos, Then you'll fall into grave trouble." The policeman looked sternly at them.

After doing the needful, Sheela and Ravi left. As Sheela moved alone in the auto, the feeling good hangover and fearlessness left her suddenly, and she felt terribly frightened. What would she tell her husband when he would ask for the report.? Just then her husband ccalled. "Sheela, where are you and what for are you doing so late? Did the report show anything serious? I hope not." Sheela was at a loss for words. However, she quickly made up a story. : "You see, the clinic was overcrowded and just when I was about to enter the chamber for my ultrasound, there was a power cut there. Something went wrong with the electricity connection there. So my ultrasound couldn't be done. Anyway, don't worry. I'll do it some other day. How's ma?"

"The operation has just been over. She has regained her senses and is in the ICU. Anyway, reach home soon." And he switched off. Thankfully, when she reached home, nobody questioned her much. Her husband and sister-in-law were physically and mentally exhausted with having to worry too much about their mother. The two sisters did night duty in the hospital while her husband returned home at 12 o'clock in the night, had his dinner, and slept beside her.

"Sheela," her husband said putting his arms around her waist. Sheela felt a bit surprised at the sudden change in his attitude. However she was too preoccupied with apprehensions about what the morrow would bring, to ponder about the sudden change in him. "I've ill-treated you a lot, but I know you've borne it bravely and with patience. I don't want you to be sick at all. Who else do I have in this world other than you.!"

"Doesn't matter at all", Sheela replied. "Everything's going to be okay. Let us sleep. I'm too tired."

But Sheela couldn't sleep a wink that night. If only that rape hadn't happened. Anyway, it was no use thinking of the past. She only prayed to God that things would turn out well the next day.

16

Ravi had flown back to Mumbai immediately after checking out from the hotel. There was a worried expression on his face, but his wife didn't bother to notice it. After dinner that night, he asked her just casually "I'm in a sort of mess. How about divorcing me?"

A thunderbolt fell on her from the blue. And she could not believe her ears. She became tense and stiffened physically, but she pretended as though she hadn't heard. "What did you say?"

"I was thinking of divorcing you"

"Why, may I know?" she thundered. "What harm have I done! Have I dissatisfied you in any way? I'll tell my father and he will punish you for saying such a thing. I'm sure you are joking."

"No, I'm not joking. I'm serious. I'm in love with someone else and want to marry her"

He looked at her straight in the eyes. Then she started sobbing hysterically. "How can you do this to me, Ravi. I, who have been so faithful to you always. God will punish you for saying such a thing. Please, please, Ravi, don't leave me".

"But I've been caught having sex with her and I've become involved in a legal case. I've no other option but to marry her"' Looking at Ravi's face, she knew he meant what he said. She stopped weeping and herself became very serious. With a grim face and rough voice, she asked, "What compensation will you give me?"

"How much do you want?"

"I want one crore rupees."

"Now come on, Priti! From where will I get one crore? You know my salary is only Rs. 40,000/- per month. As for my savings, it'll be hardly be ten-twelve lakhs. From where will I get one crore?" Ravi was aghast.

"Then give me that ten lakhs, plus 25000rupees every month. If you agree to these conditions, I'll give you a divorce. Her eyes betrayed she had no love for him at all.

"What about our son? I think you'll agree that I should keep him." Ravi knew she wouldn't agree.

"O no! never! Thank God he's asleep. Henceforth, I'll never let a characterless and treacherous father's shadow ever fall on him. He'll be with me for ever." And she strode away into the bedroom angrily and latched the door from within.

Ravi went to the drawing room and lay on the sofa. His thoughts flowed to Sheela. What if Sheela wouldn't leave her husband.? But he was sure Sheela would obey him and do whatever he wanted her to do. He only hoped she wouldn't fall into trouble with her love-making with him. He had broached the topic of divorce to his wife lest she would be shocked when she'd know about that day's incident in rooms no. 84 and 85 in Hotel Garden Inn, but he had never expected that she would so easily agree to the divorce. He was surprised that she had taken it so coolly and had agreed to divorce him. Anyway, let me hope for the best and be prepared for the worst, he thought. He had never expected things would take such a turn. What an anticlimax to those lovely moments with Sheela! With his mind burdened with various thoughts, he strode into the adjacent bedroom and lay on the bed, trying hard to get a wink of sleep.

The next morning, while brushing her teeth, the headline news in the local daily glared into Sheela's eyes. I. G.'s son caught in a rape case. After she had finished her brushing she read the whole news, for she was curious to know what exactly had happened. It seems the lovers whom they had seen had gone into room no. 85. Just after 15 munutes of their going the young Australian lady had shouted 'rape, rape "and had set the alarm. Her husband and brother were loitering in the corridor near the room, and when the I.G.'s son opened the door, completely taken aback and baffled, they charged into the room towards the lady. When the police interrogated the young man, he swore by God that he hadn't raped and that it was a matter of consensual sex. It was she who had seduced him and impassioned him to have sex with her. But the lady denied and insisted that he had raped her.

They were taken into police custody and two days later, a fast track court would hold the trial, and its decision would be final.

At eight o'clock in the morning, her son left for school, and just when her husband had finished his breakfast, and was about to leave for the nursing home, the police tapped on the door. Behind him was another police.

"Yes, what is it?" her husband asked surprised.

"We would like to have a talk with Mrs. Sheela Bannerjee."

"What about?"

"A very important matter. Please call her, we don't have much time."

"Damn it! I ought to know what that important matter is!. After all, she is my wife." Sheela's husband expostulated impatiently.

The police said very distinctly and slowly, "The important matter is that while your wife was with her lover in room no. 84 of Hotel Garden Inn, at half-past one in the afternoon, a young lady was being raped by the local I. G.;s son in room no. 85. And that cursed young man has named your wife and her lover as witnesses against the prosecutors."

Sheela's husband glared at him fiercely. "What! You must be mad. In the afternoon, she had gone for an ultrasound."

The policeman laughed ironically, "That was only a pretext. Actually, she was with her lover at that time".

Sheela's husband's anger rose and he held him by his collar. "How dare you tell such a horrible thing about my wife. I'll kill you for this."

The policeman snatched himself away from out of his grip. "Hey Mister! How dare you threaten me like this. I'll sue you and arrest you too. Before venting your anger out on me, ask you wife." he winked slyly at him. "She has cuckolded you, man. "And he laughed mockingly.

"Sheela!" her husband thundered. Sheela hurriedly appeared from out of the kitchen. On seeing the police and her husband so angry, great fear gripped her and she started trembling from top to toe. "he's accusing you of something. Is it true?" He roared, glaring at Sheela,as though ready to devour her any moment.

"No—yes! "Sheela stammered trepidly. "I don't know."

"What! The policeman says you had been in the hotel with your lover yesterday in the afternoon. Is it true? But you said you had gone for an ultrasound."

Sheela remained quiet. He came forward and slapped her hard, which sent her head reeling."Is it true? Tell me." He thundered again.

Sheela decided to be brave. Come what may, she had to face the consequences. "Yes." She uttered feebly.

Her husband took her by her hair and dragged her inside, into their bedroom. He kicked her as though he was kicking a dog and she fell down to the floor. And then he brought out a whip and whipped her continuously. "How dare you cuckold me! You shameless woman! My mother on the operation table and you heydeying with your lover.! O Sheela, frailty is thy name, really.! And I'll kill you for this, you bitch." And the whip came cracking on her, one time after another.

"Don't beat me any more. It hurts, please, please!" Sheela pleaded, but her voices were drowned in the noise of the whip. Her sister-in-law came running in. "Dada, don't beat her so much. She'll faint. Please stop. You have to go to mother." She ran to her brother and stood in front. He pushed her away. And then the whip fell out of his hand. "I'll bring the knife and kill her." And he raged like a mad man and went to the cupboard. His sister pushed Sheela out of the room. "Run away from here. He'll kill you. The police are waiting outside to talk to you. Go." Sheela ran out, right into the midst of the two policemen. "Ma'am, you Sheela Bannerjee?"

"Yes, but I can't talk with you here. Please let us go out."

"Don't worry Madam! Your husband can't do anything to you now that we are here. You just hop into the jeep and come to the police station; we'll question you there."

Just then, Sheela's husband came rushing with a knife glazing in his hand. "I'll kill her, I'll kill her", he raged.

"Hey mister! You can do nothing to her. We are taking her with us." The police retorted.

"What!" He glared at the police, astounded, and then fell down, flop! On the sofa, as though he had fainted. He breathed and panted heavily and kept on repeating "She's become a prostitute, she's become a prostitute, the bitch!", nodding his head this way and that and beating his breast. "I'll never let her into my house again, never!"

"Dada, cool down, cool down. Okay, she'll never come again. Everything will be okay, calm down a bit, I say". His sister held a glass of water and tried to pour it down into his throat while all the while massaging his back.

The policeman. with Sheela behind them approached the jeep; just then, Sheela'gaze fell on the lady's supposedly brother and husband who were eyeing her intently, from a shop nearby. She told the police and identified them. "we know they are her brother and husband. They were the ones who lodged the complaint that the I.G.'s son had raped her."

The S.P asked her several questions. "Did you really see the lady and her boyfriend entering the hotel in a very love-making mood.? That is what Mr. Ravi Kumar says."

"yes, of course. The lady even asked me from where I had purchased the bracelet, and she told her boyfriend to buy one for her. It seemed they were very much in love when they entered the room."

"The trial will be done in a fast track court after two days. The decision will be final. Till then you and Mr. Ravi Kumar will be in police custody, not together, of course, but in separate places."

"Why?" asked Sheela surprised.

"There's a lot of danger to your lives. The two men you saw may kill you because you are the only witnesses for the prosecution. No doubt, the hotel employees are there, but you are the key witnesses. The Australian tourists may kill you. Haven't you read today's paper?"

The local English daily was lying on the table. Sheela picked it up. The headlines news was that The Australian Embassy had accused the Indian Government of not giving adequate protection to the foreign tourists in their country. And the Indian Defence Minister had retorted that Oz citizens were killing innocent young Indians who had gone to study there. Rallies, demonstrations in India and Oz—the paper was full of these news.

"Ma'am, where will you stay today and tomorrow.? We will give you tight security"

"I exactly don't know. I can't go back to my house because my husband won't let me in. I'll ring up to a friend. If she agrees, I'll put up there for two days"

Sheela rang up to Sushma's house. Sushma's husband clicked it on. "Hello! Who's speaking?"

"I'm Sheela speaking. Please give the phone to Sushma." "Okay." And he handed over the phone to his wife

"Is it true? All that I read in the papers! Mrs Sharma was telling that you are the key witness against the prosecution." Her friend was very frank and down-to-earth, but Sheela knew she was a true friend and could rely on her.

"And that's exactly why I need your help. The prosecutors are after my life. I can't go back to my home. Please, please allow me to stay in your house for two days at least, of course with police security. I'll tell you the details later."

"O Sheela, you don't have to beg for such a small favour. I'll do anything for you. Do come here. You'll be perfectly safe.". The S.P. interrupted their talk. And Sheela switched off.

"Mrs, Sheela, please be ready to leave. The police will escort you."

The sun was blazing down upon the road, but there was a wintry chill in the air. People were moving along, so happy and carefree, and Sheela envied them. Why is fate playing such cruel tricks on me? She wondered. Her mind wandered to Ravi. And in the jeep itself, surrounded by policemen on all sides, she gave Ravi a call. "Hello! How are you?"

"Fine." There was a cheerfulness in his voice. "I've told my wife that I want a divorce 'cause I'm in love with you and want to marry you. Strangely, she didn't react too much. She only demanded an alimony. I'm glad. I'd give anything to be rid of her and be with you. By the way, those two fellows had rung me up and threatened me that they would kill us if we give our verdict in favour of the prosecuted. Let's see what happens. And don't worry. Take care of yourself.". Sheela listened intently to what he was saying and with a "Yes", she switched off

"which way is your friend's house?"

"Take a right turn into the next lane." She told the driver.

Her friend received and welcomed her gallantly, but her husband grimaced. Sheela sensed he was displeased with his wife for allowing Sheela to stay in their house. However, two police securiy assured them that they would keep day and night constant vigil over their house.

That night Sheela could not sleep well. On the one hand fear throbbed in her heart, any moment the two men may break the grill of the window and creep in and kill her. On the other hand, worrisome thoughts about her husband and son just would not leave her mind. She wanted to know how things were at her home front. The next day,in the morning, she rang up to her husband's mobile. Several times she rang up. Each time it kept on ringing long till no one clicked it open. At last, 'switched off' came the reply. Then she rang up to her sister-in-law. It rang and rang as if the ringing could have no ending. When it was the tenth time and still there was no reply, she decided to give up. On second thoughts, she frantically rang up again. Somehow, this time her sister-in-law spoke up "Didi, I'm boudi. How's everyone at home?" Her voice was full of anxiety.

"Boudi, how could you do this to us! Tell me! What harm had we done to you?" Her sister-in-law screeched from the other end. Sheela remained quiet for a second.

Then she spoke up. "At least let me know how's your Dada and my little Raja.?"

"Dada is not well. Immediately after you were taken by the police, he suffered a brain stroke, caused by a hypertension. We rushed him to the nursing home where Ma is being treated. His blood pressure shot up and he's almost paralysed and there'll be an operation soon. Boudi, you've plunged our family into despair and darkness. Raja is only crying and demanding to know where you are. What with the police making enquiries, people gossiping horrible things about us, Ma and Dada so seriously ill, we are going through a hell of a time. And only because of you, Boudi. You've been a curse on our family. Why did you do this?" She screeched and then broke down into tears, weeping bitterly.

"Don't cry, didi. Forgive me, please. I'm only worried and anxious about my little Raja. And your brother, and therefore I rang up to you. I;m sure you can understand a mother's heart."

"A mother's heart! You,a mother! Huh! A mother never enjoys herself with her lover when her mother-in-law is struggling with life and death on the operation table. You are a shame on womanhood. Don't you dare utter your Raja's name. You have forfeited your claim to him You are no longer his mother. We will bring him up. You are a witch and a bitch."

"Didi, please try to understand-—"but her sister-in-law had switched off. Painful and bitter tears, but silent, coursed down Sheela's cheeks. Indeed, I'm a horrible woman, a fallen woman, she thought. She didn't mind her sister-in-law's accusations or feel hurt about it. Her heart cried out for Raja. How much he must be missing her and crying out for her. Just then her friend entered with a cup of tea and some biscuits. "Now Sheela, I don't like to see tears in your eyes. Come on, be brave. You have to face the trial tomorrow. Don't break down with depression during the trial"

Sheela wasn't feeling depressed exactly, but somehow very frightened. The future seemed so dark, uncertain and unknown. Brushing aside all negative thoughts and deciding to ask forgiveness from her husband once the trial would be over, she tried to sleep, surrendering herself to the almighty.

17

On the day of the Fast Track court, there was a huge crowd in the trial room. ' The Most Sensational Case' was what the local media had termed it and there was a lot of hype about it. Sheela and Ravi were brought in separately, one after the other, at an interval of ten to fifteen minutes, each heavily escorted by the police. Sheela was called into the witness box as the first witness for the prosecution. Laying her hands on the Holy Bhagavad Geeta, she spoke out the words right from out of her soul and heart. ""Whatever I say is the truth and nothing but the truth.".

"What exactly happened on the 30th of July, when you and your lover went into the hotel 'Garden Inn' ", the prosecutor's lawyer asked.

"I object, my Lord" The lawyer arguing in favour of the prosecuted, shouted. "Mrs Sheela had gone into the hotel with her friend, and not her lover."

"Boy friend, you mean?"

"Yes, of course." The lawyer cut a sorry figure Everybody in the courtroom laughed uproariously.

"Objection overruled. Proceed." The judge ordered.

"Yes, Mrs Sheela Bannerjee, tell me what happened on that particular day at 1.30 p.m."

"We were standing at the counter and then the couple approached towards the counter, totally in love, laughing, joking, as though the world was well lost for them". Sheela went on to narrate all that had transpired and conferenced amongst them--herself and Ravi, the Australian lady and the I.G.'s son. The judge noted down the points.

Next, it was Ravi's turn. He also vouchsafed what Sheela had said and then the lawyer asked.

"What were you and Sheela doing when the lady was being raped?"

This infuriated Ravi. "First of all, the lady wasn't raped at all. We were in the adjacent room and we didn't hear anything at all."

"O, I see! You were so engrossed in making love that you didn't overhear anything when the young lady shouted ' help, help, rape'"

"I object, my Lord!" Ravi's lawyer shouted. "These are too personal questions which my worthy friend, Mr Sharma should not ask."

"Objection overruled". The witness for the prosecution began and the questions came pouring in. The hotel staff, such as the receptionist, server, etc were called into the witness box and were questioned by the lawyer appointed by the I.G. They swore and lied blatantly that the I.G.'s son forced her into the hotel at gunpoint, all the while threatening and blackmailing her. Another waiter said that aiming the revolver at him, he had entered Room no. 85, holding the girl by her hand and dragging her along with him. The I. G's lawyer asked why they hadn't raised an alarm, or called in the police immediately,to which they replied that the young man had threatened them that if they informed anyone, he would blow up the hotel with a detonator which he was holding in his hand. The Australian lady, when called in guaranteed that all that the hoteliers had said was true. The I.G.'s son, when questioned, was dumbfounded. He stared at everyone with a blank expression, and kept repeating "God knows, I am innocent." The trial was over, and every one in the audience was waiting anxiously for the judge's verdict. It was evident that the verdict would be in favor of the prosecutor. The post mortem report confirmed that it was a case of rape. Ravi was sitting amongst the audience. His eyes fell on the I.G.'s face who looked very crestfallen and miserable. Already, he was drowning in an abyss of sorrow. How to help him out?. In a flash of lightning, something struck his mind. He recollected that he had done a video recording of the couple's arrival deliberately to show to Sheela now and then as an example and ideal of how love can be truly enjoyed. He quickly dived his hands into his pocket and took out his cell-phone. He clicked on and on and one by one the recordings showed how the lady and her lover came; every step, every moment of bliss they enjoyed till they came to the counter was captured in the mobile." Me Lord!" He shouted, while the judge was rapt in writing the verdict in favour of the prosecutor. All eyes turned on him. "I have evidence to prove that all that these hoteliers are saying is all wrong and false, and that I and Sheela have told the truth."

The hushed silence turned into a low murmur which went around the room like ripples of wave. "Order, order", the judge banged the table. He commanded Ravi to give the mobile to their lawyer. Ravi hurried to the front,and clicking on the video of his cell, he shoved it into the lawyer's hand. The lawyer then went up to the judge and showed him the recording. It was then flashed on an enlarged screen by means of computer. Everybody saw it and then came to believe that it was not a case of rape, but a matter of consensual sex. The judge had just written the verdict. He immediately drew lines across it and cancelled it. Within a minute, the entire script of the verdict changed. The judge rewrote it and then read it out to the anxious audience. "according to article of penal code no. 456, Mr. Anil, who was accused of rape, stands exonerated. from all evidences, it is clear that the the sexual act between Mr. Anil and the Australian lady was done with the consent of the lady. Thus, according to Section 992 of the Indian Penal Code, the prosecutors and the witnesses in favor of the prosecutors will be severely punished for telling lies. This decision of the Fast Track court is final and abiding and no one can challenge or oppose it in the lower court, High Court or Supreme court."

The police rushed to nab The Australian lady and some hoteliers who had been witnesses for the prosecution. "Where are the two men, her husband and her brother?"

Someone from among the crowd replied, "while the verdict was being read, they ran out of the court room, but we don't know where they went."

Tears of joy welled up in the I.G.'s eyes. Overwhelmed, he clasped Ravi to his bosom and took both his palms in his. "Mr Ravi, words are not enough to express my gratitude. You don't know how happy I am today. Had it not been for you, my son would have been jailed." Turning to Sheela, he said, "Ma'am, I'm also grateful to you and I think I can never repay your kindness and bravery even with all the help I can give you. However, whenever you need my help, at any moment, just give me a call, and I'll be there for you"

"It's okay. Everything is God's wish. He has saved you. We are just his instruments." Ravi philosophised.

"Sir, kindly leave me home in your jeep. I'm anxious to be with my husband and son". Sheela requested.

Someone had overheard and commented, "O, a SatiSavitri! My foot! A shame on womanhood, really!" Ravi looked at the woman sternly and then turned to Sheela. "Sheela, please wait for a while. Come with me. I would like to discuss with you about certain matters, and then you may go."

But Sheela was not listening. Her face looked sad and worn out. She thought she was a sinner, having betrayed her husband and plunged him into ill-health and despair. She had decided she would go back to her husband, ask his forgiveness, try her best to revive him back to normalcy, health and happiness. And her little Raja was there. How could she live without him? She would tell Ravi that this was their last meeting and that she would devote all her time to carrying out her wifely duties to her husband. Her heart would bleed to tell that to Ravi, but there was no way out. For her son was more dear and precious to her than anything in this world, and she would sacrifice anything to be near her son, even Ravi. The I.G. broke in upon her thoughts. "Ma'am, my jeep is waiting outside. Please let us go out of this courtroom and I will personally leave you home."

Just then, Ravi pulled her hands and told her, "Let's quickly go out of this courtroom."

Outside, there was a host of journalists and reporters waiting to question them. "Mr Ravi, now that you are almost a hero having exonerated Indians from being termed rapists, do you intend to marry your heroine, Mrs Sheela.?" "Are you getting a divorce from your wife?" "Is Mrs. Sheela divorcing her husband?" "You have a son, I think, Mr. Ravi."

But Ravi was not paying heed to them. His eyes had fallen on the two foreigners, who were lost amidst the crowd and were standing at a distance. One of them was aiming a revolver at him and had just pulled the trigger. Ravi immediately bent down and pushed Sheela to the ground. The bullet hit a reporter and he fell to the ground. "The foreigners are to the left of the road and they are trying to kill us." Ravi shouted to the police. The police spotted them and rushed towards them while the journalists ran helter-skelter. Ravi picked up Sheela to her feet, and pulling her hands, shouted, "Run along with me as fast as you can. They are after our lives." Hardly had they run a few yards when an ear-shattering bomb exploded just behind them and everything was lost in flames. "Run behind me as fast as you can. They are after us".

"But where are we going, Ravi? It'll be better if we hide in someone's house."

"No one will give us an entry or shelter. Keep running."

Ravi hailed an auto-driver. "Please take us to the station. We're late for the train."

"Hop in." the driver said and started the cab.

"But Ravi, why do we have to go to the station?", asked Sheela surprised.

"You don't realise that if we stay here, they'll somehow find us out. We have to go to some other place."

"But Ravi, my husband and son." Sheela whimpered. "I want to be with them"

"Shut up Sheela,! We have to remain alive if you want to be near them Therefore I have to save you by any means. God knows if I can be able to do that. Just look through the back glass by putting aside the screen, and you'll know why I am insisting that we should go away from here."

Sheela did so and sure enough, those two foreigners were in a cab 1/2km away. The road was long and straight and she could see clearly that they were trying to identify which cab they were in.

"Bhayya, speed up," Ravi told the driver.

"Sir, how can I speed up when there is so much traffic." Nevertheless, he raced up and then reached the station. On entering the platform, they heard the announcement being made that Rajdhani Express would just start then. The train began to chug out and the forced elopers ran as fast as they could. Ravi hopped and jumped into the last compartment and held Sheela's hand and pulled her in. The train chugged along speedily and Ravi cast a glance at the platform. Almost 200 metres away, he saw the two foreigners gaping at him with their mouths open. And then they came charging forward at the speed of lightning to reach the train. Ravi was looking at them through the window and knew they could never catch up with the speeding train. But just then, another train from the opposite side came up on the adjacent railway track and they were obstructed from Ravi's view.

"Sheela, they'll catch us up in the next station and kill us. We have to act before that". He turned around and saw that she was looking pale and sick. A ghastly fear was written all over her face and she stared at him, numb and dazed. Panic gripped Ravi as he feared she would faint. "Sheela," he cried out and pulled her by the shoulders. "Don't be nervous. We have to save ourselves. Pull yourself up." Sheela woke up from her dizzy dazedness and looking at Ravi, her eyes full of faith, she asked, "Well, what should we do?"

"Just follow me as we move from one compartment to the other and do as I say."

18

It was an overcrowded general compartment, very hot and people were staring at them and wondering what a strange couple they were, with no luggage or a bag even, and talking of escape and killing. They moved along the crowded and hot bogies till they reached the 3-tier A.C compartment door. Ravi pushed the door lightly to enter, but a deep sonorous voice held him back. "This is a reserved compartment. There is no place here for general passengers." Ravi and Sheela looked across and for a second, were wonderstruck, their anxiety forgotten. It was as though they had set eyes on Wordsworth's host of golden daffodils. All the passengers were dressed in lovely yellow robes and on their heads were perched turbans of bright yellow colour. Pictures of small blooming daffodils were dotted all over their robes, and for some moments, Ravi and Sheela were mesmerised in their nervousness. Unheeding the yellow-robed man's pronouncement, they entered, and then another similarly dressed man asked them, "Yes, what do you want?"

Ravi level-headedly said, "We have just come to cool ourselves, both of us; it's very hot in the general compartment. We'll just sit for a while and then go." Within him, a terrible fear of the Australian terrorists was mounting up and he could read the same fear flitting across Sheela's face. Both were breathing heavily, and sitting down on the berth, they wiped off the beads of perspiration from their face. "Both of you look exhausted. Would you like to eat something?" A yellow-robed man asked.

"Yes, please. We are very hungry. We havn't eaten anything since 8o'clock in the morning" Ravi looked at his watch. It was already 5p.m. Thick, black clouds blanketed the sky outside and all of a sudden, it had become dark. The train sped along with full speed. At any other time, Sheela would have loved to listen to the noise of the speeding train. But now, she hated it. Each passing movement of the train brought them closer to death, for she and Ravi were sure their opponents would climb up in the next station and kill them.

"Why hadn't you eaten since 8 o'clock?", Someone's voice broke upon Sheela's thoughts. Sheela hesitated to tell and looked at Ravi, but Ravi decided to tell them the truth. "You see, a court trial was going on, in which both of us were witnesses. We just ate our breakfast and went to the court. It ended at 3 p.m and the verdict was in favor of those whom we had supported. When we came out, our opponents shot at us and then bombed. Luckily we escaped and since then we've been on the move. They spotted us as we were climbing the train and I'm sure they'll catch us up in the next station and kill us."

"You want to be killed by them? Or would you liked to be saved?" The chief of them spoke. He was a huge man, almost 7ft. in height, with a muscular frame. As he stood up to go to the toilet, he towered above all of them, his head almost touching the roof.

"No, no, we don't want to die. Please save us, please." Ravi begged of him and held his feet. He picked up Ravi by the shoulders and bade him to sit down. "Just relax and be comfortable. I'm just coming from the toilet and then I'll devise a plan.".

The five minutes that they waited seemed to Ravi and Sheela five hours. When the chief came, there was a peculiar glow in his face. He whispered something to two of his followers, and sitting down he ordered Ravi "Both of you do as you are told and you'll be saved. I think you are lovers, right?"

Ravi was surprised at his power of intuition but he just said "Yes!"

The two followers led them towards the toilet and as they passed form one compatment to the other, they were surprised at the large number of ladies in this holy order wearing the same yellow robes. From a distance, one could not distinguish them from women, but on looking closely, Ravi noticed that the womens' head dresses were mostly like scarves while the mens' were like turbans. The men and women were sitting close to each other, and everybody seemed to be happy and cheerful. Ravi and Sheela looked at each other with astonishment, their eyes asking so many questions, but they quietly obeyed the two men. They were so preoccupied with thoughts about their own safety to bother or ponder over such matters. A lady follower took Sheela to the toilet and snipped off her hair with her scissors. "What are you doing?" Sheela asked, angered. "Don't worry! We've been commanded by our boss to do that. And that too for your own safety. If you are dressed like any of us, your pursuers won't recognise you." Sheela almost wept to see to see her lovely tresses going down the hole of the toilet to waste and wither on the railway tracks. But she hid her sorrow, lest the boss didn't help them. Undressing her, the lady exclaimed, "Wow, what a lovely figure!" And then she quickly clothed her with the yellow robes. Sheela felt strange at the sudden turn of events that were taking place in her life. She didn't know what the future held in store for her, where her fate would lead her to. In the opposite toilet, similar thoughts invaded Ravi's mind as the male follower shaved off his hair and covered him with yellow from top to bottom. On coming out, both Ravi and Sheela stared at each other, feeling strange at the other's new appearance. They sat down quietly and gobbled up the chappatis and vegetable curry that was given to each of them on two separate paper plates. After another twenty minutes, the train reached an insignificant stop and halted there for ten minutes. Fear sprang up in Sheela's eyes for she sensed that her attackers had boarded the train. She looked at Ravi who assured her, "Don't be frightened. They won't recognise us."

The guard gave off the whistle and the train chugged off again. The painful, slow, struggling minutes ticked by for Sheela and Ravi as they waited fearfully for their terrorist hunters to make their appearance any moment. Half-an-hour passed away and a yellow robed man said, "Now, where are your chasers. I think they have missed their victims. They must be searching in another train." The words had hardly come out of his mouth when the door creaked and the foreigners barged into their compartment. Both of them took out revolvers from their pockets. "A man and his lady love have entered this compartment. Someone told us that and we know they haven't come out of this place. Just hand them over to us and we'll leave you alone." One of them threatened.

"No man or woman has come here." The chief replied in a gruff voice.

"Hey you, don't tell a lie." And one of the miscreants pointed the revolver to a disciple's head. Bringing his face close to him, he looked at the man closely, "Let me see if this is the man disguised as a yellow bird."

Within a fraction of a second, the chief pounced on the foreigner and snatched away the revolver from his hand. The Oz terrorist fell and immediately, the others rushed and gagged his hands and legs.

"Shoot," the foreigner shouted to his companion "and blow up the compartments" But before he could pull the trigger, a follower boxed his head so hard, that he passed out immediately and fell. "Latch the door." The boss commanded. ""Their bodies are all loaded with RDxs and atombombs. And a single false step may spell death to all of us." The foreigner tried to wriggle out of his gagged hand and leg, but the boss jabbed the silencer revolver into his forehead and shot him. He senseless companion also met the same fate, and one by one all the bombs and rdxs were nimbly taken out of their pockets and belts and carefully kept in a bag.

"Shall I throw them out?" a follower asked.

"No, you fool. Some may blast off and cause a lot of damage. Soon, we'll come to a bridge and we'll hurl these bombs into a river. Meanwhile, lift the bodies to the upper berth and lay them in a sleeping position to avoid suspicion. We'll throw them out in the river late in the night when all are fast asleep"

Ravi and Sheela felt terribly frightened. They stared all around, stunned and numbed. Never in their wildest dreams, had they ever imagined they would be in such a situation. Soon, the fearful nature of their predicament gradually unfolded before them. Meanwhile,the train sped on into the darkness of the night thundering through tunnels and rumbling over bridges which easily drowned the noise of splashes in the river made by the bodies and atom bombs being flung into the dark waters.

"Both of you haven't eaten much, I think." The chief said. "Our caterers will bring you dinner. Eat and have a sound sleep. When the TTI comes, be very casual and behave as though nothing has happened. And please, for heavens' sake, don't keep staring at the dead bodies. We must avoid suspicion." Both were too dazed to speak. They just obeyed and having eaten their dinner, they lay down in their respective berths. And though deep down in their consciousness, an unknown fear of the future was lurking behind, the physical exhaustion and the awesome events of their day were too much for their tired nerves; and soon they were fast asleep.

On waking up in the morning, Ravi glanced at his watch. It was already seven o'clock and when he looked out, he saw that the train was rushing through paddy fields and it would reach Delhi in an hour. Ravi looked at the boss, who smiled and assured him. "Everything went off smoothly." Ravi could understand that he meant the bodies had been disposed off without any hint of a suspicion being raised. Ravi turned to Sheela who was sitting beside him, "On alighting at Delhi, I'll see that you board the train to Bhubaneswar and go back to your parents. I will go to Mumbai and after completing the legal formalities for a divorce, I'll come and seek your hand." But Sheela was not listening to him. Her thoughts were far away. Would her husband forgive her, she wondered. She would return to Kolkata and beg her husband to forgive her and not to desert her. For how could she live without Raja, her sweet and only darling son. He was her life, his blood, the apple of her eye. If forgiven, she would sever all her ties with Ravi, even if it meant pain and suffering Sheela. She looked at Ravi He was talking with one of the yellow robed men. "Now that we are nearing Delhi, please give us back our original dresses so that we can wear them and get down at the station."

The man laughed sarcastically. His chief had gone to have a talk with his followers in the next compartment. "After all that we have done for you, you want to leave us? It's often that one cannot save oneself by the help of money, or disguising, or even killing. However, you are very fortunate that we were there to save you."

"We thank you profusely for it and we are very grateful too." Ravi bowed down and touched his feet paying obeisance. "And I promise I'll repay your kindness one day. But for the present, we have to go back to our families and children. Come Sheela, let's go to the toilet and disrobe." Ravi got up and pulled Sheela.

"Sit down!" The follower thundered. "Once you wear this robe, you cannot wear any other dress."

"What do you mean?" Sheela asked surprised, hoping against hope that its implications meant something not very bad.

"It means you become members of this Holy Order forever and you'll never be allowed to leave it" The follower said loudly and decisively.

Sheela broke down into tears and stared at the man in dismay. "But I have to go back. My little son is there. I cannot live without him. Please allow me to go back only once,this time; I'll just be with him for some time, in fact for the last time, and I'll come back to your Holy Order once again.

The man scowled horrifyingly. "You'll go back and tell the world that we have murdered those Australian terrorists ! And then of course the police will be behind us. Don't try to befool us, young lady. We know you'll never come back."

"Please, please, let us go." Sheela begged of him and held his knees.

He pushed her away, and she fell down on her back. "Will you stop disturbing me and irritating me?" he scolded Sheela. "One more word and both of you will meet the same fate as the foreigners." Sheela was hardly on her feet when she crouched back in fear. She wasn't afraid of dying but she didn't want to put Ravi's life in danger. Ravi looked at Sheela's nervous face, and putting his fingers to his lips, he beckoned her to remain quiet. Sitting down, Sheela put her hands on her face and wept and wept bitterly. Tears streamed down her cheeks as she told Ravi, "Just think, I cannot see my Raja any more, Raja, my wealth and life, whom I love so much. I don't know what he'll do without me, he'll just cry and cry and cry. O Ravi, tell me, how can I live without him.?" And she continued to weep.

The disciples of the Order stared at Sheela as though she was a mad woman. "Sheela, calm down." Ravi consoled. "Everything will come off well. Just have patience."

The train slowly came to a halt. It was a very crowded station, the coolies rushed up to the exit, but the men of the holy order didn't want their help. One by one all of them disembarked and stood in a queue silently waiting for a bus to take them to take them to Sannyasidham, a Himalayan town, famous for its scenic beauty and a yoga center. Sheela's sobs died down as she marvelled at the discipline of the followers, who lined up quietly behind their chief. Sheela broke the silence amongst them. "Ravi, why is it that God has always chosen me to suffer so much!" she uttered helplessly. "I think I shouldn't have carried on with our affair so far. Therefore he has punished us."

"Why do you think he has punished us? Rather I think he has helped us to be united. You should thank him and be grateful to the Almighty Lord for having saved us from being killed by those terrorists." Ravi held Sheela's hand affectionately. "Don't feel so depressd, my dear. Just think, after overcoming so many obstacles, we are together at last."

"But Ravi, can you imagine my Raja being happy without me?" She turned to Ravi with tear-strained eyes. ""must be missing me terribly". And she started sobbing again.

"Now come on Sheela, cheer up! I understand a mother's heart very well, but then, I too have a son. I too feel the pain of separation from him. But we can do nothing. We are mere puppets in the hands of the Almighty. They make us dance to their tune, pulling the strings as, when and where they like.". Ravi philosophised "Besides, all along we have been steeped in suffering the pain of separation from each other, and we have become quite used to bearing sufferings, so that we can tolerate this pain too. Now Sheela, forget the past totally, your home, your husband. Begin again. Let's wait and watch as the future unfolds before us. As for my wife, good riddance! Thank God, I'm naturally leaving her without having to undergo any legal hassles. And my in-laws are there to care for my son. Come on Sheela, smile a bit, because I know whatever God does is always for our best." Sheela wasn't convinced. Fate had been playing very cruel tricks with her. But still, in order to please Ravi, she smiled feebly through her tears. "But this dress Ravi, I hate it."

"Shhh!" Ravi put his fingers on his lips. "Don't utter a word about the dress. They may overhear and punish us. Just think, this dress saved our lives; therefore you should not hate it so much."

Soon, a huge luxury bus arrived. "Order of Peace" was written on it in bold letters. Ravi and Sheela climbed into it along with the members of the organisation and it headed off towards Sannyasidham. They slept off on the way and as they neared Rishikesh, they started shivering. It was beginning to get cold and when they reached there, the sun was just beginning to rise and it cast its golden glow all over the mountainous landscape. A calm sense of serenity and peace emanated from the purity of the white, snowy hills and it filtered into the worn out minds of the lovers and brought some solace to their souls. The 'Order of Peace' had a huge mansion there, at Sannyasidham, and into it they filed one by one. It was centrally air-conditioned and they felt quite felt warm inside. After reenergising their tired bodies and mind with food and tea and a good sleep in the afternoon, they were huddled into a jeep in the evening after the sun had set and the darkness had deepened. Seven jeeps, bedecked with yellow robed men and women started a night long vigil journeying through a labyrinth of tall oak trees, pine and cedar spread over miles and miles of the mighty Himalayan range. Up, up and up they went through the thick, black jungles and Sheela pierced her eyes into the darkness to see where they were heading. A pale moonlight shone above and Sheela could know that the way through which they were going was so narrow, streamed with bushes and small boulders that nobody except those who had traversed that way several times could ever find a way through it. Only these members of the order of peace knew the way and their jeeps groaned and trudged along these zigzag way higher and higher up the steep Himalayan mountain ranges. All through the night they journeyed and Sheela couldn't sleep well at all, fearing the jeep may tumble over into the valley any moment. The slopes leaned almost at an angle of 80 degree and Sheela marvelled at the dexterity with which the drivers miraculously manouvred their respective jeeps through the forests standing at such sharp and steep slopes. None but an expert hand could achieve this and therefore nobody else other than these men had ever dared to foray their way and penetrate into the secret and mysterious empire of the members of The Order of Peace. The biting cold wind swept through the openings of the jeep and cut into their bodies and Ravi's teeth chattered and cluttered. When the flaps were pulled, he felt better and fell asleep. Soon after, Sheela too rested her head on his shoulder, and tiredness overcame her and she too drifted away into the land of sleep.

It was 8o'clock in the morning when ultimately the jeeps stopped. "Wake up, guys," someone yelled. Sheela and Ravi woke up with a start and jumped out of their jeep. They were shivering but a brilliant dazzling sun, smiling like a Lord over the majestic mountains warmed and melted away their cold. "Wow!" Ravi clasped Sheela's hands, his eyes wild with amazement. "what an awesome wonder! What breathtaking and majestic beauty! Look at the mountains, Sheela, so wild, primitive, and yet so innocent, just like you" He shouted excitedly, like a child who has received a new gift, and pranced around joyfully. Sheela stood transfixed, spellbound, enthralled by the glistening splendour, the cliffs smacking of royalty, full of pine forests and high above, the snow capped peaks. They were on a sort of ledge sticking out of the mountains, a huge shelf on which an airstrip had been constructed. The aerodrome was so meticulously done and managed by these yellow-robed people that Sheela marvelled and wondered and felt sure that no mishaps could ever occur. Amidst such splendid beauty, the past was being gradually erased from her memory till it had receded to one corner. Three small aeroplanes, all yellow in colour, on which was inscribed in bold black letters, ' Order Of Peace' were already perched there, ready to take off any moment. "Come on, all of you first climb onto the first chopper and we shall start", ordered the chief.

19

As the flight took off, Sheela, who was sitting beside the window, felt absolutely enchanted. The bird's eye-view from atop was simply breathtaking. For a moment, she held her breath in awe. She felt as though she was entering into a wonderland and a fairyland. She felt like a bird, who had suddenly learnt to fly, speeding into the unknown, into freedom, unto joy where there would be no shackles preventing her from being with Ravi. The clouds floating by looked like huge boulders in a blue and white ocean. Thoughts of her son Raja and her husband which had receded to one corner of her mind surfaced again, but she forced herself to push it to sink and drown and become just a residue. What's the use of remembering them and feeling sad? She thought. She turned to look at Ravi and he smiled as though he could read her thoughts. "Let bygones be bygones, my dear". And Then she smiled at him and both of them uttered simultaneously "Let the past be totally forgotten" And then they laughed out aloud. They clasped each others hands and laughed and laughed, so joyous and unalloyed, like when they had laughed long ago when they had just entered into their teens, and were playing hide and seek with others, and were hiding together under a huge table, and when the spier passed by them and couldn't see them. But then, it was a noiseless laughter, but now, it was a full-throated one. They flew up and up, high above the glorious himalayan mountains, and the lovers eyes feasted on every inch and nuance of the scene. High up in a beautiful valley, measuring 5000 acres of land, nestled amidst cup-shaped mountains, they landed in a well-carved beautiful air-strip. And then, they were driven to a modern palace at the top of a hill. While journeying in the car, Sheela and Ravi stared and stared and couldn't keep their eyes off the wondrous beauty of the place. All the buildings,apartments, the gardens, the roads, the pavements were so spick and span and looked wondrous, and the lovers felt that they had reached Heaven. That such a Heaven existed high above the Himalayan mountains was unbelievable and unimaginable, but it was true. The streets, lanes and bylanes weere flanked by lovely evergreen trees, like cedar,pine and oak and everywhere one could see batches of young men and women sweeping and brushing aside the leaves and dirt from the roads. An aerial view would make these people look like blooming yellow flowers amidst lush greenery. After a journey of almost an hour which was a most exhilarating experience for Ravi and Sheela, they reached the most beautiful building they had ever seen. They entered into a huge hall, tastefully decorated, and immediately, as though welcoming them, a melodious band, played by these yellow-robed men, enthralled their ears. At the far end of the Hall, there was a throne studded with gems, and on the throne sat a lofty, strange kind of human being, the like of which they had never seen before. Almost 9ft in height, he was dressed in silken milk white robes and had a robust appearance. His face glowed with a lovely pink glow and a beatific smile played around his lips. He could be anything from the age of 50-200 years. "Welcome, welcome," He boomed, coming forward and clasping their hands warmly. "Welcome to Utopia." They were led to lovely bedecked chairs. "Sit down. Soon we'll have the oath taking ceremony. I know you must be tired and hungry. So first eat and fill up yourselves." He clapped his hands twice, and yellow-robed servants rushed to bring their food items. After they had had their fill, the oath-taking ceremony began. Musicians played a most heart-warming and enthralling band as the giant-sized man sat. And then, all of a sudden, there was a pindrop silence. "Repeat what I say." The man ordered them. They were told to put their hands on his head and take the oath. They did so and they said. "From today onwards, swear that we belong to The Order Of Peace." They repeated his words. "We will abide by all the rules and statutes strictly and live a very disciplined life." Ravi and Sheela looked at each other and said the same. "We will forget our past, our families, our children and be called Anand and Anandi from now onwards." Ravi and Sheela did not want to utter these words and hesitated for a while. But when the man shouted angrily ' repeat', they did so in a hurry. "and if we deviate from the rules and regulations of this organisation, and from what our master or Lord says, we agree to be killed immediately. Our master's word is law, our master's word is God, and we obey and continue to obey it with our mind and soul, and from the core of our heart. "They said these words distinctly and as the musicians started playing again, they bowed down and touched his feet. He put his hands on their heart and blessed them. It was a beautiful feeling. They stood there, electrified. A strange feeling, one of elation and joy shot through their blood and it was then they realised that their Lord indeed had some strange,miraculous powers. They felt rejuvenated, strengthened, and it was as though their minds were floating in a world of joy and happiness. They were given a warm, cosy and comfortable room to sleep in. All the apartments and buildings were centrally heated. The air outside was not too cold either. It never snowed there, but there was a cosy chillness in the air.

"How strange", Ravi conversed with one of the disciples as they proceeded on the road towards a one bedroom, hall,. "High above in this area, some thousands feet above sea level, there should be only ice. But its quite warm comparatively, and everywhere the trees look so fresh and green. Marvellous! Unimaginable really!"

"You see the mountains beyond?" the yellow-robed disciple pointed his hands towards the the grey and blue expanse of the hills. Ravi looked around at the entire range of mountains cupping the valley at the bottom half. The lovely valley was almost 5000 sq. acres of land with gigantic mountains surrounding it. And the top portion of the mountains leaned in the sky towards the centre of the valley at a great height so that the upper half of the range formed a triangle pointing towards the sky. No wonder such a beautiful place was hidden from the outside world because the top portions of the mountains formed a sort of steep roof over the entire valley and somehow insulated the lovely valley from the extreme cold outside. "This bounteous and remarkable valley is entirely the brainchild of our Great Lord. He roamed about all the mountain ranges of the world for almost two years and ultimately he found this wonderful place. The mountains forming a kind of roof protect us from the bitter cold outside." Ravi looked up as far as he could and indeed strained his nape in doing so, and saw only a small portion of the sky through which the sun filtered its bright rays into the vast expanse of the valley. The brilliance of the white and blue sky matched so well with the grey and green of the mountains that it was a dazzling play of colours. Ravi marvelled at their Lord's genius at discovery. "But how did we come in ? The space above looks so small.!"

"How foolish you are! It's not at all small. There's enough space for an aeroplane to come in and go out. Because it is so high up, it looks small.

No outsider going in flights can ever locate this area. To them, it seems just a continuous range of mountains and forests."

"Are there no mountain passes here.?" Ravi asked surprised.

"No, there are no mountain passes here. This wondrous place is absolutely impenetrable except by means of an aeroplane." And then the follower's voice became excited. "At such a great height, every nook and corner of the mountain tops are filled with glaciers round the year. But look at this particular place! How beautiful it is.! Miles and miles sprawling with lush greenery" His eyes glowed strangely and reverentially. "By our Great Lord's miraculous powers, he converted this icy terrain into the most fertile region in this world. I tell you, if there are two crore varieties of herbs, plants and trees in this world, everything grows here."

"But from where does the money and man-power come to do all these activities?" Ravi asked surprised.

The man laughed. "Most of the people here don't know what money is nor have they seen a single rupee. They grow their own food by means of agriculture. For their clothes too, they do extensive cotton plantation and breed silk worms too. And you see the lovely apartments we have providing us shelter!" His eyes shone with a peculiar glow. "Food, clothing and shelter, and even consensual sex. What else does a man want! Our Great Lord gives us everything". There was a huge statue of their Great Lord nearby, beside the road and he prostrated himself reverentially before it. He then ordered Sheela and Ravi to kneel down and touch the Great Lord's stony feet.

Sheela's eyes grew wide in wonder. "What about the palatial building at Sannyasidham? Many of you stay there too, I think."

"Yes, some of us do stay there. We market our Naturopathy medicines from there. We have grown a variety of plants there too out of which we make medicines and sell to the outside world. Our Organisation makes millions out of it but not a single pie comes up here. All business and financial matters are transacted at Sannyasidham. Actually all our medicines are manufactured here in our lab, but people of this world know that they are done there at our centre at Sannyasidham"

"Do the people of the earth know that you have an empire here up in the mountains?"

"No, nobody except those belonging to the organisation. You see, our mansion at Sannyasidham is just on the outskirts of the town and the mighty Himalayas rise up from there. And the slopes of the hills from there are so thickly forested, full of dense jungles and so steep too that no outsider ever dares to venture into it. We start our journey to the airstrip below from where you came by flight, from our mansion at Sannyasidham, by big jeeps, and always in the night time when it is quite dark. It's almost 500 kms from the base to that airstrip and it takes one almost ten-twelve hours by jeep. From the airstrip, it takes a two-three hour journey by flight to come up to this place. And if by any chance, any outsider who does not belong to our organisation comes to know of this place, either we bring him forcibly here, or we just kill him leaving behind no clue at all." Anand and Anandi looked at each other and a tremor ran down their spine. The man smiled reassuringly at them, with a warm affection in his eyes, quite in contrast to the manner in which he revealed the frightening details relating to his organisation, "Don't worry, we will never kill you, for we know you can never get out of this place; rather you'll become so used to this place that you won't feel like leaving this place at all. I tell you, it's a heaven on earth." For a moment, the newcomers thought they had come to another planet, but then they realised that this was only a small, but unique portion of the earth and that these yellow-robed men were not aliens, but a little more than ordinary human-beings and their Lord was indeed a super-human being, in fact, the most superior human being in this world, but unknown to the world. As if, in answer to their thoughts, the man continued. "Its all the brainchild of our Great Lord. Glory be to him. May he live for another one thousand years.! So that he can asquire more and more knowledge". And he knelt down and lifted up his hands and looking up, he seemed to thank God.

Ravi and Sheela were struck dumb. "One thousand years! Can a person live so long?"

The man stood still and stared at Ravi. "Why not? Do you know what is his age?"

"I think he must be seventy years old."

"Seventy years old? You know nothing really. Our Great Lord is already more than two hundred and fifty years old. Two hundred and fifty!" he repeated, emphasising the number. "Most of us here are almost a hundred years old." Ravi looked at him astonished. "But how come all of you look so young.?"

The man's eyes filled with reverence. "By the grace and benevolence of our Great Lord. He's a miraculous man, I tell you. Do you see the small hill there?" he pointed his fingers far beyond. Ravi and Sheela could see only a cluster of trees over the hilltop. "That is the Hill in which some Sanjeevani plants grow. If a dying man eats even a leaf of that plant, he'll become alive. But if one dies of bulletshots, the leaf will have no effect."

Ravi and Sheela listened to him, their eyes wide with amazement. "And far away is a garden containing trees which exudes so much warmth that even big glaciers nearby melt away. And our Great Lord has bordered the entire valley with these trees and this creates a warm greenhouse effect which totally prevents the icy coldness outside from penetrating into this lush green terrain." His eyes were inflamed with awe and adoration for his Lord. "He is a genius really, where plants and trees are concerned. Not even the greatest botanist in this world knows that such kind of trees exist. Outside the valley, beyond the green mountains, the temperature is -500 degree celsius. And you know, life cannot exist in such coldness. There is only ice and ice everywhere. Outsiders do not know such a place exists at all. And even aeroplanes or jets going to and fro from foreign countries, never venture into these skies. Because it is so very cold and high too,and they are afraid they may dash against these mountains. But here, inside this valley, it is so pleasant, perhaps only 9 or 10 degree celsius. Don't you think it is a miracle indeed.!" The man continued to sing praises of his Lord, and the couple listened to him, feeling more and more strange in this wonderland. The follower showed them their room and as they entered some followers brought in two sets of dresses and robes for Ravi and Sheela and just after they had gone, they saw groups of men and ladies towards these several one-room apartments. "Why are so many ladies coming together?" Sheela was surprised. "Today is Wednesday. This is the only day in a week when the ladies are allowed to meet and sleep near their lovers. Marriages are not held here. Our Great Lord does not believe in rituals. Our Lord believes that too much of sex or expression of love will hamper the quality of our work so they are allowed to meet only on Wednesdays. Everyone should do some kind of beneficial work or the other, and there should be some kind of discipline in one's life. Any deviation from rules will cost one's life. There have been many instances when our Lord has shot and killed some of his followers." He looked at them meaningfully, suggesting that they should be strictly bound to the unwritten rules and regulations here. A strange fear crept into their hearts, but sleep had started crawling into their tired bodies and they started yawning. The tremendous leap to such an advanced and high level of space and time within one night had totally exhausted them both physically and mentally and much as they wanted to listen to the wonders of the Lord, they couldn't, for their eyes just drooped by themselves. ""Okay, now both of you take rest and I am leaving". After he had gone, both Sheela and Ravi plunged into their beds and lay close to each other. "Sheela darling, what a strange adventure, really. I had never imagined we would be together again at last. Anyway, I thank God for it."

"Yes, I'm grateful too. But Ravi, the past keeps bobbing up to the surface of my mind now and then. Pictures of my little Raja. I really miss him a lot."

"O Sheela!' Ravi intervened. "Forget the past and let us enjoy the present. Come, let us make love."

"No Ravi, please. Today, I'm exhausted. We'll do it next Wednesday. I'm sure you don't mind, do you?"

"Not at all,dear. Your happiness is my happiness." And he laughed joyfully. "I'm also very tired. Let us sleep." And hugging Sheela fondly, both of them drifted away into the world of balmy and delightful slumber.

20

In the morning, they were awakened exactly at 6 a.m. by a loud blaring horn. And then started their day's routine—6-7am,morning ablution and bath. 7-7.30, pranayam, 7.30-8am, meditation, 8-8.30, yoga, 8.30-9.30, breakfast and from 9.30 onwards work and work till 1 pm. From 1p.m-2p.m, lunch and from 2-4,a short nap and then rest. And again, from 4-8 work again. The ladies worked in the kitchen and men in the agricultural lands. Anand was given work in the computer department. There was also a small hospital, but rarely did one fall sick and the lone hospital mostly catered to delivery patients. Two blissful years passed away so quickly for Ravi (Anand) and Sheela (Anandi), like a flash of lightning, like a speeding train running smoothly. After two years, Sheela also gave birth to a lovely cute son of Ravi's and their joy knew no bounds. They were always grateful and thanked their Lord for bringing them together, and keeping them together too. Each day was an adventure as they delved deeper and deeper into love, discovering and realising the power of it, the joy of it and the wonder of it. Many times, between 2-4p.m, they met in the green and yellow paddy and wheat fields and folicked about gaily in the sun, wind and rain. **One day Sheela woke up very early in the morning at 5 a. m and she wanted to feast her eyes on and bask in the glorious beauty of the marvelous mountain scenery and watch the sun rise up higher and higher. Far away, she could see the pass which was the gateway to the mountains. On one side, it looked down on a huge wide grassy plain, and on the other, there was a little valley,and beyond,** the mountains rose up higher and higher to the eternal snows of the horizon. Just then, Ravi came up from behind and stood beside her. She had told him the previous day to come to the appointed place so that they could enjoy the scene together. Sheela ran to a lovely lake in the wide plain and Ravi ran after her, as though chasing her. Then panting heavily she sat down on the grassy bank and, gazed at the white mist hovering over the water, then rising into the air, and leaving sparkling drops of dew on the green carpet. Silence reigned everywhere. But soon, the rising sun awakened all creation, the groves and the shrubbery came alive, the birds took wing and burst into songs and the flowers lifted their faces to imbibe the life-giving rays of light. Waking with the birds, Sheela and Ravi rejoiced in the morning together with them and Sheela's pure, joyful spirit shone in her eyes as the sunshines in the dewdrops. There was a general joyousness in nature which was very infectious, and it attacked them gently, coursed through their whole blood and entered into their soul. They were floating in a heavenly ecstasy. Ravi looked at Sheela with tenderness in his eyes and took her hand—and Sheela stood there with downcast eyes, burning cheeks and fluttering heart, unable to pull her hands away, unable to avert her face when he brought his lips close to hers. Yes, he kissed her, kissed her so passionately and ardently that to her the whole world seemed afire. "Sweet Sheela, I love you." And these words were echoed in the depths of her soul like heavenly sublime music; she hardly dared to believe her ears but her shyness vanished in that moment of rapture and Ravi knew that he was loved passionately by this, pure and open heart. It was the most beautiful experience in his life, a new, unalloyed happiness. And this kind of an unending joyous and happy living increased in them the love for learning. And everyday, they learnt something new about their work and acquired more and more knowledge about it. The desire for learning, the craving for it, became the driving force in Ravi's life and all of a sudden, life appeared to be more meaningful and worthwhile with Sheela beside him. And more than anything, he wanted to learn the art of Sanjeevani from his Lord, just for the joy of learning and nothing else. Ravi and Sheela came to know more about the greatness, grandeur and greatness of their Lord's mind. He could have easily conquered the world with his knowledge of Sanjeevani and be the wealthiest man on earth. No, he did not. He shunned money and hated amassing wealth. Whatever money their organisation earned by manufacturing cosmetics and herbal medicine, was just enough to make his people live in a simple way with high thinking. For the work which his people did in the farms, in the kitchen and in bringing up children, as in managing computers, they were never paid money. Instead, all were allowed to live in the same manner of comfort, eat the same food and wear the same clothes. Thus, there was no competition and hence no greed, and children were nursed and brought up by a special team of men and women who took the utmost care of all of them. Of course, their natural mother and father could sometimes go and visit them, but their upbringing was totally left in the charge of these specialized group. The Lord deliberately kept his knowledge of Sanjeevani unknown to the world. He knew that if he declared his knowledge to the world, greedy and cruel human beings would not allow him to live in peace. They would come to know of his secret world or hideout and then spoil its virgin beauty. He was well aware that to get the secret of Sanjeevani or immortality out of him, they would at first woo him, and then when he wouldn't yield, they would capture him, threaten and even go to the extent of killing him. He knew that human beings were greedy animals, and before they could get his hands on him to learn the art of Sanjeevani, he would be compelled to kill them. But he did not want to spoil his hands with unnecessary murder. Besides, it would be worthless labour getting into trouble with them, and therefore he hid his secret of the knowledge of the Sanjeevani from the outside world. Thus, he lorded over some ten thousand people in a beautiful world high amongst the steepest mountain ranges of Himalayas and only now and then, he spread his Message and Order of peace to the world outside and beyond. Another important information also Anand had come to obtain; that The Great Lord had a natural daughter, only 30 years old, who was born and brought up in the U.S.A. After her mother had died when she was fifteen years old, she had come to stay here in her father's regime up in the Himalayas, but she had never liked it here. These days, she lived in the U.S.A., and very rarely did she come here. He had also come to know that she was a paragon of beauty, but not yet married; and still searching for the right man to marry. These yellow-robed men and women never gossipped, nor did they speak ill of anyone;for it was not in their code of conduct or habit to do so, but somehow Anand was able to pick up this much information from stray conversations here and there.

The Great Lord liked the man Anand, and of late, he had developed a special fondness for him, and was thinking of teaching him alone the art of Sanjeevani lest some mishap may occur to himself any moment and the knowledge may well be lost to the world.

And then one day when the Spring season was at its peak in the beautiful valley, while it was an icy world outside in the mountains, while the flowers bloomed and the nightingale and cuckoo sang sweetly hidden in the branches of the trees of the valley, and the small streams danced their way merrily down the luscious green slopes; on one such day when Sheela was reaping the golden grain and the sun's rays dazzled her face, Ravi came running towards her and said, panting, "Anandi, come with me, I have something to tell you.". The time was 11.30 a.m.

"How come you've left your work in the computer room and come here?" Sheela asked surprised.

"Well, my legs and neck became stiff sitting there since 9o'clock and I wanted to enjoy a bit of fresh air too. My thoughts naturally went to you. Come, my dear, let's go and enjoy ourselves a bit.". He winked naughtily. "You know what I mean" There was a childish fervour in him and Sheela realised that the joys which they could feel, enjoy and imagine when they were children had suddenly revived itself in them; she was surprised that now she could laugh and smile so easily and naturally. She knew that living simple, innocent lives high up in the mountains,without any money to promote greed, free of hassles, stresses and tension had made them young, jolly and cheerful once again, like they were once long ago in their childhood and teenage.

Sheela pulled him aside, away from the other women. "But Anand, our Lord may know. Besides, someone may see. You know, it's so open everywhere." Ravi laughed; the laughter which had dried up in him ever since he had entered teenage, burst forth in him once again like a brook laughing its way merrily over the pebbles as it courses its way through the hills. "Our Lord likes me very much. I'm sure he'll excuse me a little dalliance with my special and only beloved in this world." Ravi came forward and pulled her hand. "Come, my dear, let's make a little love" and he pulled her arm. Sheela threw down her sickle and followed him. They went behind a haystack and suddenly he hugged her close to him and kissed her on her lips. "Come, lets make love hidden amongst the grain. Its so romantic and I can't wait till the next Wednesday." He took out his yellow robe and stood thee, with only his undergarments clinging to his body. Sheela stared at his virile and manly body, tall and muscular, glistening in the sun, and her libido went shooting up and she came forward with open arms intending to embrace him. But he wasn't looking at her any more. He was staring up, his eyes glued to something at the top of the haystack, and her eyes followed his gaze. Like Anand, she too stared and stared, dumbstruck and spellbound. She was looking at the most beautiful woman she had set her eyes on. "Wow! What a beauty!" Ravi gasped. They were surprised to see that she wasn't wearing a yellow robe. Dressed in dark blue jeans and a colorful flowery top, with a hat tilted upon her shiny golden hair, she looked the perfect picture of Marilyn Monroe, the famous Hollywood star of yesteryears. Surprised, Ravi aimed a tirade of questions at her. "Who are you and where have you come from? How come you are dressed in formal clothes.?"

She laughed loudly and her ringing laughter echoed in the valley. "I'm your great Lord's only natural daughter." She was wearing boots and she jumped down from the haystack with a great thud, and then came closer to Anand. "You see," she smiled ironically, "I was conceived in my mother's womb by your great Lord in a fit of passion, and then he forgot about my mother and me. Then, he didn't even know that I had been created. My mother was just beginning her career as an actress in Hollywood, and since he no longer met her after that, lest he could not achieve his greater mission of being the Lord of the Universe, she died of drugs and depression when I was only fifteen years old. And you know, whem I claimed my daughterhood, your Great Lord even tested my DNA. As if I would tell a lie." Her face sqirmed in disgust and hatred for her father. "My mother used to spend sleepless nights, crying in her dark loneliness, and I never forgave or will ever forgive your so called Lord for this." And she looked at Anand with sinister eyes, throwing away her hat.

Her thick brown hair caught the sun's rays and dazzled while her marble like white skin shone and glazed in the sun. Anandi and Anand thought she was a fairy descended from heaven—so beautiful was she! Anand kept on gazing at her unable to keep his eyes off her. For a moment, the whole valley seemed to be bathed in a strange silence. Then her tinkling laughter showing beautiful even white teeth broke the silence as she eyed Ravi's bare body minutely, taking in all the details. "Wow! How handsome you are!" she ejaculated excitedly. And then she leapt forward and tried to hug Ravi. Ravi backed, taken aback. "What are you doing!" he asked angrily.

"I want to make love to you", she laughed dangerously. ""O God, man, I've fallen in love with you and I want to marry you." And she pranced about wildly. "you really look so handsome, like a Greek God, an Apollo." And again she kissed him lightly on his cheeks.

Ravi pushed her away, but she was very strong and heavy and did not budge an inch. Ravi was furious. "I won't marry you. I love Anandi and I'll never betray her because I cannot live without her."

She turned at him with fiery eyes. "How dare you say that! If you once again say you love her, I'll shoot her dead. Look, I have a revolver. And I know my father cannot revive people who have been killed by bullet shots." She took out a revolver and turned to Sheela.

"And my dear lady, never try to meet Anand again. We are starting for U.S.A tomorrow morning itself." She almost dragged Ravi and his legs carried him away, as though he was moving on wind. She seemed to have the strength of a lion, and however hard he tried to pull himself away, he couldn't. She eyed him cruelly. "How dare you try to run away from me! You know what! It's only because you are capable of loving someone truly that I have fallen in love with you Otherwise, where physical strength is concerned, you are no match for me. And if you make a greater fuss, I'll kill your dear dear Anandi." All of a sudden, Ravi felt very frightened. A shiver ran down his spine. What if she really killed Sheela? He was traumatised and obeying her meekly, he followed her as she almost dragged him by his hand

"Papa", she stormed into the Hall, pulling Ravi beside her, where her biological father was sitting on a huge throne, surrounded by some of his yellow-robed followers. The Great Lord gestured to his followers to leave the place and after they had filed out of the Big Hall, he turned to his daughter. "Yes, what's it? What new whim has obsessed you again?"

"Papa", she shouted. "I want to marry this man". And she pushed Ravi forward. "but since there's no marriage ritual here, tomorrow I'll be flying to the U.S.A. via Delhi, and I' ll take him with me. There I'll marry him and you must do this for me."

"Cool down, Little Baby, and try to be reasonable." Her father gently chided her. "He loves Anandi and will not be separated from her. Why don't you understand that he doesn't love you at all? Besides, he has no passport or visa. How can he go so soon?"

"Papa", Little Baby stormed. "you never wanted or cared for my happiness. You've never loved me nor are you capable of loving any one at all because you are passionate about power. You've given me millions of dollars, estates and properties in the U.S.A, but you've never given me love. Papa, I'm fed up of money, properties and estates. I'm hungry for love and love and love." She screamed, pulling her hair. Anand stood there, trembling, frightened of her hysteria.

"Calm down, Little Baby." Her father tried to pacify her. "Allow me to ask Anandi once. I don't want to hurt her feelings or be unjust to her by waiving off her opinion."

"How dare you utter her name in my presence. You know she's my rival and I hate her." Little Baby roared and raged, stamping her foot. "She has nothing to her credit in comparison with me—neither looks, nor beauty nor wealth; yet Anand loves her madly and will do anything for her, even die for her sake. And that is precisely why I want to marry him, because he is capable of loving someone, which quality as far as I know,no man possesses Amongst all the people in the world, he's the only man I've found and know who is capable of true love, a pure pure love. Everybody else, including you too, Papa, are greedy, deceitful liars and selfish, and therefore I've fallen in love with him. He's undoubtedly very handsome too." Her face, all of a sudden, lit up with a smile, and shone with a peculiar glow. She turned to Ravi, "We'll marry in the U.S. A. in great pomp and splendour; after that you'll be mine forever until death do us apart and I'll teach you to love me and me alone." She turned to her father. "Now Papa, don't tell me that he can't go ; how he'll go is your lookout. He can easily pose as any other yellow-robed man who has a passport and a visa. And mind you, Papa, I won't take 'no' for answer. If you deny this pleasure and happiness to me, I'll kill myself. So bye"! She turned and pulled Ravi along wih her. Ravi looked back pleadingly at his Lord, his eyes beseeching his Lord to prevent his going, but to no avail. He realised Little Baby was the apple of his Great Lord's eye and all sense of morality failed in him where her happiness was concerned. At night as he lay on the bed with Little Baby beside him, his thoughts wandered to Sheela (Anandi). How strange! Fate always conspired with time to separate Sheela from him. He was sure Sheela would be crying her heart out by thinking of the possibility of living away from him. But never for once did he imagine Sheela would take it in her stride. It was true that initially, on seeing Little Baby's possessiveness over Ravi, a tinge of sadness struck her; but after some time, her sorrow faded away naturally. Life, or rather fate, one should say, had presented itself to her with so many strange experiences and uncertainties that she no longer felt troubled at the unforeseen or unimagined events of her life. She had learnt to accept these and in that she felt a great sense of peace. The only emotion she had felt vibrantly all these years was love for Ravi, alias Anand, and that gave her a great sense of joy. She felt she was lucky indeed to experience and enjoy true love which is one of the rarest thing in this world; for Ravi had given her so much love all these years that just the memory of it would suffice to make her energetic, joyous and vibrant for another one hundred years. Besides, there was Ravi's cute little son who was a great source of joy, rather a bundle of joy whenever she picked him up in her arms. He looked exactly like Ravi and she loved him all the more for it. She hoped Little Baby would love Ravi, alias Anand and thus gain his love and affection. Somehow, she felt reconciled with fate and fell fast asleep that night.

21

When Sheela woke up in the morning, it was 5.30 a.m. She had overheard that Ravi and Little Baby would leave at 6 a.m. She had a great desire, a yearning to have a last glimpse of Ravi before he left for the States; for she knew that Little Baby would never allow him to come back to the Great Lord's land ever again. But she knew it was dangerous to go, for if Little Baby would see her, she would harm her and hurt Ravi; therefore, without a word to anyone, she quietly slipped off, and rushed to a small wood near the airstrip, and hid herself behind a tree. Hardly had she waited for five minutes when she saw them coming—Little Baby, the Lord, Ravi and some followers and the entire crew of the aeroplane. Little Baby, dressed in red formal jeans, looked like a rose in full bloom amongst the yellow robed leaves and branches of the men of The Great lord. Sheela, alias Anandi, peeped from behind the tree to catch a final glimpse of Ravi as he climbed the staircase attached to the door of the aeroplane with Little Baby holding his hands tightly. He was not clearly visible to Sheela, but as if by telepathy, she could sense his gloom and unhappiness. Just then, Ravi caught sight of Sheela. For a moment, he stood still, thunderstruck; then he flung off his VIP suitcase, and shouting "Anandi, my Sheela", he broke free from the clutches of Little Baby and ran forward with joy, shouting, "Sheela, my Anandi, I'm coming back to you".

Little Baby stood rooted on the staircase,shocked beyond words. "Anand," she screamed, "Come back, I say, come back, I order!" But Anand turned a deaf ear to her howls. Sheela was too frightened. Words failed her, but impulsively she ran away from Ravi, fearing Little Baby might kill him if he reached her.

"Anand, come back, please. You can't betray me like this." Little Baby raged on and on. But Ravi ran and rushed as fast as he could in order to reach Sheela, all the while shouting, "My Anandi, I'm coming to you. Don't go away from me."

The Great Lord stood dumbstruck, like a statue. "Papa,!" Thundered Little Baby, rushing to her father and shaking him. "Shoot him, I say. He has betrayed me; please Papa, if you don't, I'll slit my throat with this knife." She took out a small, sharp knife from her jean pocket and held it to her throat. He pushed away her hand and then the knife fell. She was about to pick it up again and hold it to her throat, but the Great Lord held her hand and lifted her up. Then, his face hardened, he took out his revolver and aiming at the sprinting Ravi, he shot at him. The bullet pierced Ravi's shoulder, and pain coursed throughout his body, but he continued to run. On hearing the shot, Sheela turned around and seeing Ravi's face contrite with pain, she turned around and came running towards Ravi. "Anand, Anand, I'm coming to you", she shouted. And ran forward to reach Ravi.

Little Baby screamed, "Papa, he's not yet dead. I can't just bear to see them together again. Shoot him again, I command; otherwise I'll kill myself." Again, the Lord shot at him, but Sheela came in front of Ravi and the bullet hit her. But by then, all Ravi's energy had drained away and he fell into Sheela's arms gasping for breath, blood streaming out profusely from his shoulders. Both of them fell to the ground, holding each other in their arms. There was a glow of happiness in Ravi's eyes even though excruciating pain shot through his whole body and his face contorted with extreme physical agony. But he said distinctly even through his bodily anguish. "Sheela, my dear, at last I've got you. And I'm so happy to die in your arms."

Tears were rolling down Sheela's cheeks and within her, the pain was becoming unbearable too. "no Ravi, my Anand, you won't die. I won't let you die." Her words faltered and her voice became feeble.

"Anandi, you too are dying. It must be very painful, this bullet shot, my dear. Come, let me wipe away your tears.". And while wiping, he hiccuped and said, "Fate, destiny, people, all were jealous, envious of our love, joy and happiness and always contrived to separate us in our life. Only death has brought us together once again. Henceforth,if rebirth is true, in all our lives we will be together, for love is truth and love is eternal. Bon't cry, Sheela dear, I can't bear to see you in pain. Smile, for my sake at least.

Even through her tears, Sheela smiled. "Yes, Anand, we'll be together always." She gasped for breath. It was her last breath, and then her head dropped to the ground. Just then, Ravi too breathed his last with a beatific smile on his face.

Tears sprang up in the Lord's eyes as he towered over their bodies and ordered his men to place them side by side. "Anand was a man whom I loved and trusted the most." Turning to his daughter, he asked in a voice choked with emotion, pain and despair, "Now, why did you kill him? He had never harmed you."

"Papa, it wasn't me who killed him." She screamed. "It was you who shot at him. If you hadn't killed him, I would have died. It wouldn't have mattered to you, would it? He was more important to you than me." Tears glistened in her eyes too. "Anyway, even if I did kill him through you, what's wrong in it? I loved him and that is why I hated him too; and therefore I killed him. Haven't you always preached—love and hate, hope and despair, joy and sorrow, day and night, always go together. And therefore I wanted him to die. Because I loved and hated him simultaneously". And then she laughed out aloud. Like a mad woman. "Anyway, Papa, I'm going away just now. Whenever I come, some mishap occurs. I always disturb the peaceful world over which you Lord. I promise you I'll try my best never to come here again." Then she walked away to climb the stairs to board the flight. As the plane took off, The Great Lord's gaze followed it going far away, beyond the clouds, till it vanished out of his sight.

ABOUT THE AUTHOR

Mamata Dey teaches English in a reputed Autonomous College in the province of Odisha in India. She has done a doctorate in British Literature on the dramatic works of John Dryden and is currently guiding many research scholars of English literature and language. An avid reader and an extensive traveller, she has authored two books—a novel and a collection of short stories. She lives with her husband and children at Khordha, near Bhubaneswar,in Odisha, a province in India.